The Swiss Chocolatier

EUROPEAN TYCOONS

BOOK THREE

LEANNE LOVEGROVE

Dedication

To the picturesque postcard town of Hallstatt. You are gorgeous! This story is inspired by you and the fabulous chocolate houses of Europe.

Chapter One

Sapphire Banks had never lived up to her bold name.

And yet, over the last forty-eight hours, she'd travelled by aeroplane, enduring two stopovers at the frantic and foreign ports of Singapore and Paris before arriving in the Austrian city of Salzburg. From there, she'd caught a train and now a ferry and was almost, finally, at her destination. She was quite literally across the other side of the world from her small rural town of Canungra, Queensland. Or Gold Coast; everyone knew the glitter strip but was not familiar with her hometown. She'd learned that too, on the plane and the train, talking with other passengers who were from exotic European cities.

Sapphire whipped out her phone and woke the screen. She flicked to the photograph of her white and fluffy Shmoodle, Winston, followed by the shot of her family. She'd taken them before she'd left home and had gazed at them a million times already. Each time, an ache spread across her chest; she'd expected to miss her family, but this homesickness was like a real, live, visceral pain and, frankly, hard to bear. Flicking the phone off, she placed it back in her bag. Constant staring at her loved ones would not make this situation any easier.

The small ferry boat bobbed gently with the rocking of the waves as it made its way across the wide lake. On each slight rise and fall, Sapphire's eyes closed. Having never travelled overseas before, exhaustion had seeped into her bones and settled there. The extent of her fatigue meant she could curl up right now and catch a few minutes of sleep. No one had warned her that jet-setting across the globe was so tiring. On the next dip, her lids shuttered shut again, but as the boat crested the next wave, she opened them to a picture postcard scene.

Had she fallen asleep and was now dreaming? Rapidly blinking her eyes in quick succession, she double-checked that the scene in front of her was real. What she looked at, was, dare she say, perfect. Quite possibly the most gorgeous town she'd ever seen. But that wasn't saying much because she hadn't seen many places.

However, in this instance, the guidebooks were right. The glittering blue dazzle of the water met blue and tangerine-coloured buildings that bordered the lake but crept high up the incline, covering the side of the mountain towering in front of her. It was exactly like a scene from *The Sound of Music*. The homes had balcony flower boxes, and they bloomed in shades of colour, adding even more beauty to an already incredible scene. Her lips curled into a broad smile that spread across her face, her spirits rose, and the fatigue that crippled her slipped away.

Picturesque Hallstatt was renowned for being the most beautiful town in Austria and perhaps Europe. She had done that homework. And she was here. Sapphire couldn't believe it.

A quick glance at the other tourists revealed they weren't quite as enthralled as she was, but nothing could quell her enthusiasm. She wanted to soak up every detail. That didn't stop the nerves bubbling up inside her at what lay ahead.

In only a few minutes, she was about to land and spend the next three months of her life living in this community. Imagine if her accommodation had a flower box! Her mother and sisters would love this place. She might suggest her mother install flower boxes on the rustic cabins they hired out for rent on their property at home. That would help create the cute and romantic atmosphere her mother desired. Except home wasn't triangular rooftops with matching-shaped window frames in a mixture of colours. Home was subdued rolling, green hills, roaming wildlife and suffocating Australian heat. Funny, that was a great analogy for her; Sapphire was subdued and comfortable like her small hometown with its cute cafés and farms and down-to-earth folk. Nothing like this town. Who would she become here? Would she become dazzling like the great lake or colourful like the houses? Would she finally live up to her name?

Sapphire twirled the gold bangle she wore around her wrist. Enough of that defeatist talk. She'd come, she was here, and she was proud of herself for that. She'd be the first to admit she hadn't wanted to travel across the world and was reluctant to accept the opportunity thrust upon her. But how could she have refused? Turning down the offer of a mentorship with the most brilliant and talented chocolatier in Europe? Unheard of, even she understood that. Who'd be so stupid? Not her; she coughed into her hand. But she would never, ever have been so courageous as to have applied in the first instance. Hence why her kind employer, Seb, had done so on her behalf.

Sapphire recalled his excitement, the palpable thrill when he delivered the news. His eyes lit up as he'd told her she was chosen from thousands of applicants to live in Austria for three months and be taught by one of the best in the world.

In the end, two things had persuaded her to accept the challenge: one, she'd do anything for her boss and his company. They were like a second family to her and had given her a job and trained her to be the chocolatier she was today. Perhaps not the best in the world, but she made some decent chocolates at the factory in Canungra. *Hinterland Chocolate* was a wonderful business to work for. And she owed them; times had been tough and she'd do anything to make them great again. Secondly, she'd do pretty much anything for chocolate. It was her life. Had become her life, well, after...

Sapphire Banks would be okay; she could do this.

The boat arrived at the dock where a crowd had gathered. Glancing back over her shoulder, the lake they'd traversed appeared ginormous, but they'd crossed it quickly. Sapphire faced forward, got ready; this was happening...finally, she was here. She shivered as the sun disappeared behind the mountain range and the vessel stalled in a shady patch. She tugged her lightweight cardigan tighter around her. It was early September and the locals had only just kissed goodbye to summer. Shouldn't it be warmer? Or perhaps it was nerves? Either way, she hoped she'd packed the right gear. Something else to worry about.

The boat knocked against the terminal, and the passengers around her flurried into action. Men on the shore lugged large ropes and tied the ferry securely. Sapphire took her time, stood, and stretched her arms above her head while nerves took flight in her belly. She lifted the handle of her wheelie case, lifted her handbag higher onto her shoulder and scanned the crowd. People hugged, cheered and greeted friends and loved ones. No one seemed to be looking for an Australian girl travelling alone. Lobbing down the internal ferry steps one at a time, she waited for the crowd to disperse and moved across the gangplank.

Safely on the other side, the crowd parted, and she spotted a man holding a white sign with her name in red. He leaned casually against a timber fence and gazed at his phone.

Thank goodness! Sapphire released a breath in relief and picked up her pace as she manoeuvred around the gathering of people until she paused in front of him.

The man glanced up, his lips forming a smile so wide that his cheeks creased at the edges of his face. Sapphire's breath caught, and she stepped back. She hadn't known what to expect from the locals, but this guy appeared more Italian than German, with his dark wavy locks resting on broad shoulders and a shadow of yesterday's beard lining his square jaw. Yep, good-looking in any language.

'*Guten tag,*' he said, deep, guttural and low.

'Hi,' she replied, accompanied by a quick wave.

'I am Marcus.' The broad grin never slipped from his face, pearly-white teeth on display.

'You speak English.'

'*Ja, natürlich.* We all do.' He winked!

'Do you speak German?' he asked as he reached for her case.

Sapphire shook her head, unable at that precise moment to form any words.

'That's okay,' he continued, his tone turning somewhat American, 'you'll be fine. Everyone here speaks some English.

And if you have any trouble, you can ask me.' His cheeky grin was matched with sparkling green eyes. 'Let's go, I'm taking you to your accommodation.' He moved away across the terminal, and she hastened after him, madly twisting her bangle.

'Oh, and,' he swung his body around to face her once more, 'congratulations on winning!' He turned back away, not requiring a reply.

A moment of apprehension gripped her. Could she survive in this foreign place not only out of her comfort zone but in an entirely other stratosphere? She guessed she'd find out soon enough.

Chapter Two

James took a bite of the small square of chocolate; it was smooth and creamy with a hint of cherry mixed in with the dark, bitter cocoa. He opened his mouth to savour the decadence once more . . . reached for it—

'James.' Long and slender fingers traced up and down his bare arm, causing goosebumps. 'James.' The sexy voice was as velvety as the chocolate he'd been dreaming of.

He opened his eyes, and when he rolled over to face Valentina, she offered him a come-hither smile.

She pulled him in close until her breasts rested against his chest, and her legs curled around his body. 'Come with me to Milan; it'll be fun,' she purred.

'No.' It came out more forcefully than he'd intended. He sighed. 'I've explained I can't leave at the moment—'

'Won't leave, you mean? It's the weekend! Only three days —' Her tone softened until she realised it wasn't having any effect. 'You don't have to work weekends. You have a whole team to make your precious chocolate. Plus, it's only a few days. Please?' She batted her eyelashes seductively and trailed her fingers once more across his skin.

'No,' he said again and meant it. James removed her hand. 'I can't. It's not the weekend yet; it's Friday, and that's a workday. Even for me.'

Valentina emitted a groan of frustration, unravelled her body, and rolled away from him, leaving her naked body on top of the white cotton sheet. It was hard not to desire her, she was perfect, but his phone beeped with the arrival of a message. A timely reminder it was time to work. He twisted away and retrieved the phone from the nightstand to read the message. Engrossed in work, he was reminded of Valentina's presence by her hefty sigh.

'What time do you leave?'

'In a couple of hours. I'll need to head off soon.'

'Coffee first?' he asked.

'Of course.'

James rose and walked naked to the bathroom. 'Are you sure you don't want to come back to bed for a little while?' Valentina crooned, but he shook his head and kept walking.

In the kitchen, he ground the coffee beans, and while waiting for the machine to warm up, he checked his emails. Valentina was speaking rapid-fire Spanish to someone on her phone before her arms snaked around him. She nibbled his ear and pushed her naked body against his back.

Today was the day their new and first-ever mentee arrived. The project, or scheme, if he was being droll, was designed by the company to boost their profile and to demonstrate their desire to share industry knowledge, give back and be an all-round good global citizen. The applications had come from all over the world, the reach far greater than they'd expected, the competition fierce, and James had no idea what to expect. Would he get an amateur who had no idea about chocolate and wanted to kickstart their career or someone with experience trying to climb the corporate and social ladder? He didn't know. He wasn't sure it mattered. He'd deliberately left it to his well-paid and experienced PR team to sort the details. But now, it was his turn to act. His team had delivered on their promise, and today was the day he, as the recently appointed CEO of Grindelwald's chocolate factory in Hallstatt, would meet the lucky recipient. It was to be a carefully choreographed meet and greet as they made chocolate together while being filmed for the company's YouTube channel. He wasn't apprehensive about it. James White didn't get nervous, but it would be hell working together for three months if the person was a dud.

'I've got to go, no time for coffee. Our flight has moved earlier, and I've got to pack,' Valentina murmured in his ear; the sensation tickled rather than seduced him.

He liked Valentina; she was good fun, drop-dead gorgeous and sexy to boot. They'd spent some fabulous nights together, drinking too much and welcoming in the dawn. But when he needed to work, which, unfortunately for her, was frequently, she was an unwelcome distraction. To make this newly refurbished and branded local branch of the chocolate factory great, he needed focus. And that meant fun was left to the fringes of his time.

There was no need to be mean though, so he spun on the spot, surprising her with a long, hard, deep kiss. She took it as an invitation; he meant it as a farewell. He unwrapped her arms and held them by her side. 'See you when you get back,' he said, kissing her quickly once more before moving to collect his double espresso and read more emails. He didn't notice her leave.

Standing at the granite marble island bench in his kitchen, feet wide apart for balance, he sat his coffee down, not wanting to ruin his palate. First, it was chocolate—always the chocolate.

In front of him was a selection of small pieces, slithers of what the factory had handcrafted only twelve hours before. Fresh, room temperature and delectable-looking.

He took his first bite. The chocolate melted on his tongue; James tasted the flavours and they blended nicely. It was good, but James wanted great. He'd only recently taken over the locally run chocolate factory and turned it into a Grindelwald conglomerate, and only the best would do. The standards of the international brand were high.

In between bites, he swished water in his mouth to cleanse it before reaching for the next morsel. It was the same. And the next. He'd tried to avoid drastic change at the factory in the early days of his management. Still, it was proving tricky to incorporate local ingredients and new staff into their well-established and tested Grindelwald recipes. They weren't quite there yet; the distinct flavour expectation had yet to be achieved. And it had to be. James drank his espresso in one gulp.

Did he have time to work on it now? Tinker and manipulate, create something amazing? Practice and perfect? His fingers stretched in and out as he stood in his industrial kitchen designed specifically for chocolate making. He had an entire factory, but he loved nothing more than crafting in the quiet and solitude of his home. He wanted to be able to make chocolate whenever he felt like it.

Another message arrived; the decision was made. Anyway, he needed to be in the factory demonstrating to the staff. Plus, his team waited for his arrival to be prepped and ready for the special introduction this morning. There'd be plenty of chocolate-making ahead.

With her eyes clamped shut, Sapphire swung open the cabin door. She had no idea where she was or what the time was. But the loud banging had to stop.

'*Scheisse.*' One foreign word and her world crashed back down around her, and she instantly remembered that she was in Hallstatt. A group of people stood at her open door, mouths agape and their eyebrows shooting towards their foreheads. Matched with those expressions, she assumed the German word wasn't a pleasant one. This was confirmed by their next phrases in perfect English.

'Oh boy. We've got some work to do.'

Multiple bodies pushed past her and rushed inside.

The light was bright, and Sapphire squinted against the glare.

Daytime! Morning! 'Shit! What's the time?' she asked, her voice raspy as her arms braced against the doorframe for support.

'Relax, sweet cheeks.' A hot mug of coffee was shoved into her hands.

Sweet cheeks? But she recognised that accent and glanced up in time to catch Marcus winking at her.

'Oh, no,' she moaned. Her head was heavy like lead, and she had to force her lids to remain open. Her hands flew to her bed hair, softening what she knew must be an out-of-control mess. Then she glimpsed a splash of bright pink, and her hands lowered to her body in a pathetic attempt to cover up her fluorescent pink boxer pants and white singlet pyjamas.

Marcus stared with a goofy smile. 'Drink the coffee, you'll feel better. They say the jetlag after coming across the world is bad.'

Jet lag? Yes, that's what it was! Her mind was foggy as if she'd downed too many tequila shots, but she hadn't left the cabin after her arrival yesterday. And as for a big night, well, she hadn't had one of those, well, since before...

The realisation that there was a reason she felt like she was swimming upstream in a fast-flowing current made her feel immeasurably better. That was why she had slept so deeply and late into the morning when she should have been up and getting ready for her big day.

Following Marcus into the small living area, he introduced her to the team. 'This is Lina. She's head of PR for Grindelwald's and is running this campaign.'

Sapphire shot them both a quizzical look. 'I didn't realise I was a campaign,'

she said, catching an exchange of glances between the pair.

'Lovely to meet you, Sapphire. I cannot wait to begin working with you. What Marcus meant is that we've been preparing for your visit and mentorship for months with meticulous planning. And now you're here! We are very excited. As you know, today you will meet the head of the company, our wonderful boss, and the head chocolatier who will mentor you over these next few months. I'm sure you are familiar with the schedule, but we're throwing you right in at the deep end. That is what the English say, yes?'

Sapphire nodded, uncertain of what she was getting at.

Lina didn't notice. 'We have the first session today, which is also the meet and greet, and it's being filmed—'

'Filmed?' Sapphire's throat threatened to close.

Lina laughed in a false tone and waved her hands around. 'It's only for the company's YouTube channel. Don't worry. We have quite a few subscribers, and we're trying to build the platform. There might also be a few magazine journalists present, too. Anyway,' more hand swishing, 'to ensure you look your best, we've brought in a team to help you prepare.' Lina waved her arm wide to encompass the room that was now filled with additional bodies and their styling equipment.

A woman prepared brushes and capes and plugged in a blow dryer. A man set up an enormous makeup case. Sapphire was stuck on the words filming, magazines, and the need to prepare. 'Gosh, all of this is for me?' she asked, taking another sip of coffee, but now she wanted that tequila.

'Of course. Marcus, get Sapphire another coffee and a selection of breakfast that we've brought with us, and we'll get you set up over here.' Lina pointed to a wing-back chair set up at the kitchen basin to wash her hair.

'Or I could take a shower?' she suggested with a shrug.

Lina laughed, a lighter tinkle this time. 'Don't be silly. We are doing everything for you.'

'And this is for my first meeting?' This simple catch-up

sounded like much more than she'd anticipated. Being mentored meant their workplace was the kitchen, didn't it? She was expecting to be shown how to improve her skills in the craft of artisan chocolate making.

Plus, as anyone would, she'd stalked her mentor prior to departure. Not that there'd been much to uncover. There was only one old, staid photograph of a man on their website who looked like he was one hundred years old and rocking a white beard like Santa Claus. His image didn't promote him as innovative and as one of the world's best chocolatiers, but hey, who was she to judge? Other than that one image, there was nothing else available about the renowned chef apart from his impressive work history.

The team from Grindelwald was acting like this was a very big deal and had Sapphire's anxiety notching up. What was the fuss? Had she underestimated what she was getting into? While the head chocolatier resembled an old grandpa, his team were young and hip. And why was it being covered by the press? Couldn't she turn up nicely dressed? Her clothes would be covered by an apron anyway, right?

Too many thoughts raced through her mind, and panic set in. Taking three deep breaths, she willed herself to relax. The old Sapphire would have dreaded being primped and pampered until she resembled someone else. But darn it, she wasn't at home now, and she was about to meet one of the best chocolatiers in the world. Perhaps during her time in Hallstatt, she could become someone new, or at least an improved version of herself. Now, that was a thought.

She lowered herself into the chair and dreamed of chocolate.

Chapter Three

A thrill raced up James' spine as it always did when he entered the factory. The aroma came first: cream, followed by malt and a hint of vanilla, then the atmosphere. The noise of the machinery quietly hummed in the background, as did the chatter of talking. These sensations combined, and adrenaline raced through his veins. This generation spoke of finding your tribe; James wouldn't go that far, but this was his place. His chocolate factory is where he was happiest. If he was honest, it was where he most often wanted to be. It's an unhealthy obsession, but the truth.

'There you are,' Lina, head of his PR team, rushed forward, flustered and out of breath. Her stiletto heels click-clacked on the polished concrete floor as she approached. 'We've been waiting.'

He held up his palm. 'Not yet, Lina. I've only just arrived. I'll be with you in ten minutes, I promise.'

Her mouth opened and shut. She knew it was useless to

argue with him, and he was glad she didn't bother. Lina nodded silently and walked away.

James entered the factory and swore that for a moment, time stopped. All eyes craned towards him, breaths held, and the production line was forgotten. Seconds passed until the conveyor belt rattled again, and eyes returned downwards. Staff resumed their normal routine.

He moved to the first station and spoke in German to the staff manning the line. His language skills were rudimentary at best, but he'd mastered the basics. The women smiled coyly while the men nodded sombrely without pausing their work. Being an enigma was not new to him. Here, the local Austrians hadn't entirely worked out their new owner with his funny accent. They thought him British, but his lilt didn't make sense, nor was his skin pasty and pale like those from across the Channel. Yet it wasn't his confusing looks that had the staff flustered. James made no apologies for running a tight ship; he was strict, and regulations had to be adhered to. There were no excuses; the chocolate quality was always paramount. Strict but generous was his mantra. Reward for hard work was high on his agenda, and diligent staff who kept his chocolate to the high standard he aspired to would reap the benefits.

Plus, a little bit of mystery couldn't hurt. Soon, he was sure, they'd match his passion for chocolate; if they didn't, they simply wouldn't fit in.

He caught his expression in the shiny metallic surface of the bench. It was severe, and he turned the corners of his lips into a smile.

But his appearance on the shop floor didn't mean he checked on his staff or their progress. It was his indefinable need to control, along with his desire for perfection and consistency, that drew him into the dens of the chocolate-making world every day. There were no German words that could convey this sentiment. The chocolate had to be perfect; that was his job. The signature chocolates wrapped and placed into packages and neatly trimmed boxes were about consistency, something the customers expected. Regardless of whether it was their artisan, individually handmade chocolates or their boxed sets, the taste and experience had to be the same each time a customer purchased a Grindelwald product.

Moving across the main floor, he offered waves and greetings to the staff and stopped at a station to collect one of their signature stars. Closing his eyes, he held the small, unwrapped shape under his nose and inhaled. Bitter. Sweet. Sugar. Cocoa. It was all present. Opening his eyes, he turned it each way and examined its smoothness, its curved edges and perfect symmetry. It was glorious. He nibbled one corner, and it was warm on his tongue. Divine, he would never tire of the taste of chocolate. But still, those doubts lingered...

'It's perfect,' he said in English to the closest worker.

'*Danke*,' she replied, keeping her smile while continuing to work. He popped the remainder of the chocolate into his mouth and glanced up to catch Lina as she paced near the factory door. When he was within reach of her, she tugged him by the elbow towards the front room where the team had gathered. No one else dared to boss him around in this manner, but that was why Lina was so good at her job. Excitement pulsed around the room, making the air electric. His staff were as thrilled as he was, but perhaps about different things.

James looked for the mentee but saw only familiar faces. 'Where are they?' he quizzed.

'Well, we've been waiting for you. We've decided your first meeting will be on set.'

Apprehension stirred in his gut, but he trusted his team. They'd worked hard on this project.

'Okay,' he nodded as he was gently pushed down into a chair, hands reaching to primp his hair and powder being brushed across his cheeks. He laughed good-naturedly but swatted their hands away, standing to command the room. 'There's no need for all of that. Tell me, instead, about our candidate.'

'If you'd read the fully comprehensive dossier I'd prepared, you'd know all about her.'

James had the decency to appear contrite. 'I'm sorry. Since taking over the business, it's been all hands on deck, ensuring a smooth transition. But that is why I've left this task in your very capable hands. I trust you with this project; it was your brainwave, after all. And I know you will have chosen the perfect person without any help from me.'

Lina's shoulders dropped, and she smiled. He was forgiven. 'Well, it's a young woman who has been working as a chocolatier for some years now in a small, pretty much unknown factory on the other side of the world. Her application was meticulous, and her passion for the craft of artisan chocolate making shone through. Oh, and she's Australian like you. We thought that was a nice touch and great for publicity and promotion.'

A member of the team slapped him on the back. 'An Aussie,' they said in a terrible attempt at the accent, 'Will you know them, boss?'

Australian. The word reverberated in his head. An Aussie like him.

The walls of the room closed in.

James White had been away from "home" for the past five years, and he did his very best to avoid thinking about where he came from, the country of his birth. Sometimes, he even forgot he was Australian. It was easy to mix in over here on the continent with the multitude of cultures and countries. Everyone thought he was English anyway, and he rarely corrected them. But now memories rushed back at him so quickly he couldn't capture them, and his head began to throb.

His phone rang, and he answered it without hesitation. 'What? Fix the problem and tell them we need the supplies delivered today. Do it.'

James ended the call. While he was distracted, hands returned to fly around his face and fix stray strands of hair. Swatting them away again, he checked the emails that popped up on his screen.

'It's time. Can you please put your phone away?'

He held up one finger. 'One second . . .' He finished sending the email to head office, glanced pointedly at Lina, and placed the phone in his back pocket, where he'd feel a buzz if another message arrived.

Lina straightened his tie and ran her hands down his already uncreased, deep blue collared shirt. A voice from behind yelled, 'Boss! Can you please check something on the line?'

James' adrenaline spiked, and he stepped towards the employee. Lina was quick and caught his arm in her grip. 'Not now. I know you are the head of the company, and responsibility ultimately ends with you, but ask another member of your management team to sort it out.' Her eyes pleaded with him. 'This mentoring program is important, too; we've been working towards this moment for months. It's going to be great for you and the factory.'

Pulled in two directions, James paused. He wanted to fix whatever the issue was on the production line, and needed to ensure nothing stopped the manufacture of their chocolate. He also needed to be an active participant in the mentoring program. The program he'd agreed to, and had thought a great idea until it pulled him away from his real work.

Nodding at Lina, he shouted instructions at the employee, and the swing-back doors opened to the kitchen. Bright, flashing lights blinded him, music blared, and bystanders clapped as he entered. This wasn't quite how he had imagined it, but hey, it would look like a spectacle on their TV channel.

Lina's voice boomed around the room before her hand was on his back, moving him forward. James stepped towards the modern galley kitchen. In the shadows, a person approached from the other side of the long bench.

'Jamie?' a soft female voice spoke. He knew that dulcet tone.

The music stopped, and the room went silent. A vaporising cloud hung from the ceiling and slowly descended with gravity, draping him in a shroud of smoke. It cleared, and she emerged.

'Sapphire?'

His gut spasmed, and his mind swam. His voice carried a tinge of wonder and rose a pitch. The past he had run from caught up with him in one fast, felling swoop.

'Jamie?' she said again.

But it couldn't be. Not here. In Hallstatt. Not her. No.

Turning briefly, awkwardly, back the way he had come, he sought refuge, help. The assistance he sought didn't arrive. Instead, he spun back to face her; his feet propelled him forward towards her, his body acting on instinct. He wanted to embrace her and simultaneously push her away, far, far away. He did neither of these things, and the moment expanded. Sapphire stepped forward, and he matched her, one hand extended as if to greet her, but it hung in mid-air. After so long, she was here, standing close. She looked different. Smooth and ironed hair when it had always sat flyaway and wispy. Her olive-green eyes were moody with heavy bronze make-up, her cheeks glittering in the lighting. Pale pink lipstick painted thin lips that were stretched into an uncertain smile. Her hands clasped across her body as if for protection.

He licked his lips but maintained his gaze, unable to tear his eyes away.

Sapphire held a hand to her chest, covering her heart in the mauve floor-length dress she wore. A ridiculous get-up for making chocolate in the kitchen, but he knew she would never have chosen it, even though she looked stunning. With her mouth slightly open, she stared at him until her eyes scanned from the tip of his head to his torso and back. Her shoulder-length blonde locks moved almost indiscernibly as her head began to sway from side to side.

Sapphire spun on the spot, searching frantically for something or someone. At what must have been a last resort, she turned back to him. 'Jamie . . . you're not the CEO of Grindelwald. Where is he? The old guy from the photograph on the webpage? He's my mentor...'

Titters erupted from the small group gathered, and his

former name whispered on lips, the name no one called him except Sapphire Banks, his ex-fiancé. The one he'd left behind.

The shock of her being in his chocolate factory hit him full force in the gut.

'You're one of the best chocolatiers in the world?' Her tone was mocking.

His back stiffened, and his eyebrow arched. 'You don't think that's possible?'

Now, there was more forceful head-shaking.

'I know nothing about you anymore . . . I am here at Grindelwald to be mentored by one of Europe's best choco-latiers, the CEO. Is this a joke?' Her words caught on a stran-gled-sounding sob.

Lina whispered off-set, and he remembered where he was. A switch flicked; he braced his shoulders, stood tall and extended his hand for her to shake. His once big, bold voice filled the room. 'Welcome. I'm James White, the recently appointed new CEO of Grindelwald...'

Chapter Four

J ames? Since when had he been addressed by his formal name?

'. . . head chocolatier . . . we're very excited to welcome you, and we are confident this will be an amazing opportunity for both you and our company.'

Sapphire watched the flip. From Jamie, the local Aussie boy she'd once loved, to James. The professional, rich, and successful head chocolatier of one of the most thriving chocolate brands on the continent.

If it had been anyone else, she'd have been impressed. But it felt as if he'd slapped her, and all the air left her body.

If they'd stayed in touch, none of this might have been a shock. But they hadn't, and Jamie had never been on social media. For years after he'd left, she wished he were. She'd scoured the internet for any news of him. There'd been nothing personal, only a few minor employment announcements when he'd been promoted to a new position. The last she'd heard, he was becoming a sensation in England, touted as the next best thing. At her lowest points of stalking, she realised how unhealthy it was to try and keep track of an ex-fiancé who didn't want anyone to know where he was or what he was doing. It was painful, but she'd had to let go.

So, for that reason, she'd completely missed the information that he was now working on the continent and was the newly appointed CEO of the company that had offered her the mentorship. They obviously hadn't updated the website either. What were the chances? Did Seb know? He couldn't have; he would never have set her up like this.

The cynic in her assumed the universe was playing a very nasty trick on her.

Sapphire had dreamed of their reunion many, many times. In her wildest imaginings, it had never played out like this. Those daydreams always included Jamie's apology, followed by a declaration of love and the seeking of her forgiveness.

And now he was here.

Bulbs flashed, and Sapphire was manoeuvred into position so her body aligned with his behind a high kitchen bench. Their closeness was suffocating, and she clenched her fists so tight that the blood must have stopped circulating. 'Smile, *fraulein*!' Sing-song commands were directed at her. Jamie's stiff body stood next to her. His arm brushed hers, and he shifted it quickly.

While the bulbs flashed, she observed him out of the corner of her eye. He was the boy she remembered, except a much slicker, smoother version, like a male model from a fashion magazine. He wore suit pants with no jacket, only a business shirt secured with a tie. Strange chocolate-making attire. His dark hair was longish and curling at the top as if he hadn't had time to have it cut.

As if!

He probably had personal barbers coming to his home. Sapphire controlled the smirk her lips wanted to form. After all this time, she wanted to mock him. Revenge was a nasty beast and not at all her style.

His gaze remained fixed on the barrel of the camera as he continued speaking. This allowed her heart to settle and her ragged breathing to return to normal. Then the familiar ache in her chest returned, an ever-present longing. Wishing, the what-ifs and could-have-been. She might be surprised right now, but gosh, she'd missed him each and every day since he'd left. The sight of him, here in real life, was enough to knock her for six.

The room around her disappeared, and she fixated on Jamie's mouth. On the lips that used to kiss her all over, adore her, find her sensitive spots and make her laugh. The words he spoke washed away, but a tingling sensation rocked through her body, and she jiggled her legs to disperse it.

Until, uh-oh, the room went quiet, and all eyes focused on her. She'd missed a cue. Plastering another grin on her face, she glanced at Jamie. Her expression must have given her away as he repeated the question.

'Have I ever made hand-crafted artisan chocolate?' She gazed at him dumbstruck but saw the twitch in the corner of his left eye. Of course, he knew the answer; they were playing a game, a game where they'd only just met.

Becoming a champion at the fake full grin, she replied,

looking directly at the camera. 'I have made some, but none, I'm sure, as good as what you produce here at Grindelwald.' Jamie's shoulders relaxed, and he described to their imaginary audience the dark chocolate sea salt delight they were going to prepare in this first session.

Together, they made a show of washing their hands and donning identical black aprons, gold-trimmed and emblazoned with the factory name across the breast. Jamie dropped three small china dishes against the granite, where they made a loud clatter. Seeing him frazzled bolstered her own reserve, and she gathered her defences. All she had to do was get through this ridiculous charade of making chocolate; even if it took every-thing out of her, she was determined to hold it together. On the surface, anyway.

Sapphire wrapped the blanket more tightly around her shoulders and pressed play again. It was torture, but she couldn't stop watching the YouTube video. The footage had already been viewed thousands of times in the short fifteen minutes it had been loaded, but she guessed she accounted for quite a few of those.

Each time Jamie appeared on the screen, she swooned, and with every viewing, she cussed and swore, wishing she didn't react that way, and each time she vowed not to. It was an invol-untary reaction to how gorgeous he was. Those dark, compelling eyes that matched the chocolate he ate, the broad shoulders that fit snugly in collared shirts, the smooth skin of his chin that he'd once worn stubbled. Damn, how she wished he wasn't so alluring.

And that voice. Honestly, Sapphire had listened to Jamie speaking a bunch of times already, and she remained glued to each word. What he said was of no interest; it was PR spin and advertising on the virtues of Grindelwald chocolate. But his accent had changed; it no longer had a familiar twang. It was a formal mixture of British and Aussie. He spoke the King's English! But at each spoken word, a shiver raced up her spine. He didn't speak in German, and she found that interesting. Perhaps the company would dub it? And if he was serious about making this branch work, wouldn't he speak the local language?

Hitting the screen of her phone, she paused the film. Always the same spot, same facial expression. That moment when Jamie first saw her, the recognition hit. It was innocence, surprise, and shock, but there was the tiniest hint of something else. His facial features softened for a moment, his eyes tender and loving until the mask came down. It was the Jamie she used to know. The Jamie she loved. And it lasted only a split second. Time had stretched and then stopped until they were suspended together.

Angry, hot tears rolled down her cheeks and landed on her bare legs, crossed over as she sat on her bed in the cabin. Rain pummelled the tiled roof and frosted the windows. Pressing play again, she watched the remainder of the video and promised that she'd not subject herself to it again.

Last time.

His transformation hurt. The turning of Jamie into James. Or was this only for television? Or for his staff who watched on? Had Jamie turned into this person?

The switch had been quick, and perhaps no one had

noticed. She had, though, and he had too. The visible change in his tone of voice, the transformation was from the guy-next-door to the officious and authoritarian CEO. Very different, but it was so quick. Now, as she kept re-watching the footage, she searched for the tiniest detail of the man she'd once loved.

Would viewers care? Probably not. Maybe they put it down to a blunder, miscommunication, filming nerves, or a glitch.

But when had this transformation occurred? When he left? And why? Sapphire had loved the former version, had adored him, and everyone had. She couldn't correlate the man in front of her with the one who'd trailed his hands down her body many times and kissed her so passionately that her toes curled. But forgetting about the desire they'd shared, he'd been a good guy, the bloke next door, the local kid who had loved her.

Who was *this* guy?

A shiver shuddered through her body as she watched the mask come down once more. It was not only quick but calculated and bereft of emotion. His eyes had glazed, and recognition of who she was had disappeared. Is that what he now thought of her? Did she mean nothing after all this time?

Of course, she understood that couldn't happen on film, but wouldn't that have made a funny and whimsical moment? *Oh, hey, my mentee is someone I used to know (the lyrics of the song sprung into her head),* and Jamie could have laughed, made a joke, and agreed that they had a lot to catch up on. That's what the old Jamie would have done. But yes, Sapphire agreed it might be too personal. However, perhaps he could have taken the stance that they'd once worked together and what a thrill it was to be back together once more.

Maybe she was being too harsh? After all, she had lost the

ability to speak at the moment and hadn't been able to string a few words together, and he might have felt the same. They'd had a moment . . . hadn't they?

Sapphire wanted to hate James White. Truly hate his guts. Deep down to her very core, she wanted to despise him for leaving her, and for not loving her enough to stay. But, more so, she hated herself for not being enough to make him want him stay.

Stopping the video, she Googled James White, his formal name, and included the title, *chocolatier*. Over two years ago when she last searched him, there had been one or two hits, one of them a news article about the amazing new chocolate chef in London. Now, her screen was filled with images. Flicking through them, his face stared back at her in hundreds of photographs. In most of them, he wore suits and was in the arms of gorgeous waif-thin women dressed in couture gowns; there were many more of him in chocolate factories wearing an apron and a white chef hat, as well as some of him surfing and snow skiing.

The hick country boy had turned slick. All smooth edges with tailored clothes and meticulously preened hair. And those were the people who surrounded him. Paparazzi shots caught him climbing out of Lamborghinis and Porsches and on the arms of women decked in sparkles. There were some advertising promos for men's eau de toilette and Armani suits. And the shots were taken around the world, but mostly in exotic countries of the continent.

Holy shit.

Sapphire sighed and looked up at the ceiling. She'd known he'd become successful but hadn't quite imagined the pictures in front of her. James White was a millionaire; one of the best chocolatiers, operating a branch of one of the most successful chocolate companies globally. And he'd only left Australia five years ago. Boy, he'd been busy. No wonder he'd been so keen to break free from the shackles of their insignificant rural town and small local business and make his mark on the rest of the world. And he'd done it, she'd give him credit for that.

Scrolling through more images, one dark-haired woman appeared frequently in more recent shots. In some photographs, they stood next to each other, posing in front of nightclubs, galleries, and fine restaurants; in a few he admired her from a distance, while in others she was draped suggestively over one arm or leaning in towards him, her ample breasts revealed in a low-cut dress. She wasn't in any photographs before he arrived in Hallstatt.

Great, he had a glamorous new girlfriend to fit in with his new glamorous lifestyle.

Sapphire bit her bottom lip. She didn't want to cry anymore. He wasn't worth it. Enough tears had been spilled over Jamie— *James White*. She threw her phone beside her on the bed and pulled her knees up to her body, rocking back and forth. That old familiar ache returned, the wound in her chest that festered and filled up with want, need and pain. It hurt. It had hurt when he'd left, and now it was worse. She'd loved him, really loved him, and her heart had been shattered into a million pieces when he'd left. It had taken years to reduce that soul-crushing, life-transforming ache into a dull throb. Now it was back with a vengeance, and the fragments of her heart that had loosely realigned were breaking apart once more.

She couldn't go through this again.

Jamie had moved on to a better, different life and had forgotten about those he left behind. It was one thing to dream of her long-lost love from afar, but having him, his success and his girlfriend thrown right in her face . . . she couldn't do it. The prospect of falling apart again was too much of a risk. Leaving was the only option. Her boss would understand under the circumstances.

Yes.

She jumped off the bed and let the blanket fall to the floor, and quickly wrapped her arms around herself. Preoccupied with other things, she'd forgotten to turn on the heating, and the cabin was freezing. But she didn't need to worry about that; she was out of here anyway.

Racing around the small space, she threw her belongings back into her case not caring if they crumpled or became a higgledy-piggledy mess. There'd been no time to unpack properly anyway, so it was easy to stuff everything back in. The more she shoved, the more determined she became. Yes, coming here had always been a stupid idea; she'd given in, gone against her usual practical decision-making, and convinced herself to live a little. Well, that's what happened when you went against your gut and tried to be someone you weren't.

Exhausted, she sat back on her haunches and surveyed the mess. It didn't matter; nothing mattered, she couldn't stand by and be part of Jamie's new life. They couldn't be mentor and mentee and play a charade for the world to watch.

A knock sounded at her door. Sapphire glanced out the window and discerned through the mist that the daylight was fading, casting the room into shadow. She stood and checked the time. Seven o'clock. Maybe she wouldn't answer it? She didn't know anyone here, so it had to be the marketing team or someone from the factory. She hoped it wasn't Marcus with his winking eyes. But then there was another knock. Maybe the person wouldn't go away; they might worry if she didn't answer. Sometimes her sensible nature bored even her.

Chapter Five

Sapphire swung open the door—and immediately regretted it.

No. No. No.

She clutched the frame with one hand but retreated, creating as much distance as she could between herself and Jamie.

Jamie paid no heed and lunged forward, one hand snaking around her back to keep her in place and the other gripping the base of her neck as his lips zeroed in and locked onto hers.

There was a split second of shock, but then ecstasy took over. In less than a nanosecond, she was swept back in time. His taste, his smell, the feel of him rushed back at her with high speed and, oh, how she loved it. It was like home and where she belonged. What she had dreamed of for eons; finally, that deep-seated longing was met, her heartache disappeared, replaced by a crescendo of joy that hurtled through her body. Matching the force and pressure of his kiss, Sapphire closed her eyes and lived her dream.

Until she didn't. Until she came to her senses. Her eyes flicked open, her mouth covered by his precious lips stalled, and her body tensed. She pressed her flat palms to his chest and pushed him backwards, hard, until his body landed against the door frame.

The jolt to his back made him pause, eyes wide and stunned. His fingers moved to touch the corners of his lips that had only seconds before smothered hers.

'What are you doing?' she whispered.

Jamie looked down at his feet, away across the darkening landscape, and then back at her. Again, Sapphire sensed a switch, from old Jamie to new. His bravado had grown in their years apart. She could tell that James White was a man used to getting his own way.

Instead, he shrugged.

He shrugged!

The action incensed her, and rage built within. She placed her hands on her hips, ready for battle. But her spike of anger didn't last as he stood there gazing at her like a loveable Labrador —sort of goofy and floppy-like, uncertain. He was like the guy she had once known. She softened her stance.

'You've done all right for yourself, haven't you, Jamie?' she said, and he flinched at the use of his old name. Sapphire touched the corner of the denim jacket he wore, matched with designer blue jeans and leather dress shoes. With trembling fingers, she caressed the tips of his curly locks which she discovered were fastened securely in place.

'You never used to use hair products.' It was a stupid thing to say, and she wanted to gobble the words back up. Jamie didn't respond.

The whole situation was incredibly weird; they were both lost for words and wrapped up in a time warp.

'I'm sorry I didn't stay in contact.'

'Are you?' Cynicism crept into her words. 'You were too busy living your new and fancy life to worry about us back at home.' More sobs threatened, and she moved away from the door, returning inside the cabin. It took a split second, and then he followed.

Inside, he scanned the room. 'What's this? Why are you packing?'

'I'm leaving.' Sapphire wanted to punch the air, celebrating her bravery.

'No, you're not.'

Faced with his opposition, she crumbled onto the small double bed in one saggy heap. Unfortunately, he sat next to her. Immediately, she shifted further to the right.

'Please,' it sounded like a plea. She knew she couldn't maintain this tough demeanour. 'This isn't going to work. I can't be your mentee, I can't be here, please let me go home.' Her tone was soft, and gentle, her eyes watering.

With one finger, he lifted her chin to face him as he turned side-on towards her. 'I can't...'

She wrenched her face away, making her hair swivel around her shoulders. 'Can't, or won't? You're the boss and can do whatever you like.'

He shook his head. 'Sapphie.' Her pet name; it almost undid her. 'I can't. We've been planning this project for months. It's specifically designed to be beneficial for both the company and, of course, for you.' He paused, but she didn't speak. 'Yes, I'm not going to lie; it's a carefully designed marketing campaign to lift our local profile and attract new customers and lovers of chocolate. We're trying something different. It's been arranged for months, we've advertised. We can't back out now; it would be a disaster.'

She understood; she wasn't a completely heartless bitch. 'Okay, I get it. Get a new mentee; someone else to slip into my shoes . . . I agreed to be mentored by one of the best chocolatiers in Europe, not by my ex-fiancé who left me years ago...' She couldn't finish.

'I am one of the best chocolatiers in Europe.'

Honestly, she couldn't tell if he was being serious or jesting, but his face contained no hint of amusement.

'. . . and I happen to know you.'

'Know me? Know me?' she repeated with rising intonation.

Jamie stood up swiftly and paced the room. 'Okay, stop. I know I'm messing this up. I've been caught by surprise.'

'So, you didn't know I was your mentee?'

He looked at her and shook his head. 'I left it to my team to organise, and they chose you from thousands of applicants.'

There was something about his tone that made her believe him.

'But Sapphie, this is important to me, to the business . . .'

It was on the tip of her tongue to lash out at him. She owed him nothing! He left her and pursued his personal dreams over and above their joint goals. They'd loved each other. But none of these words came out.

'It's not ideal, I get it. I understand.' Damnit, his voice was like honey dripping down her throat. Yes, she'd pushed him away earlier, but she wanted to be back in his arms, kissing each other all over, but not like this. He didn't want her; he needed her for commercial reasons.

She paced the room in the opposite direction, running her hands through her hair. 'The best thing for me is to leave. This isn't about me; this is a PR stunt to make you money.'

'Hmm, sort of. It's also about finding new talent and improving your skills. Can I help do that?'

The cheek of him. He assumed she needed help. She paused her steps across the small circumference of the cabin. But that was exactly why she'd come, right? To learn something, anything that she could take home. Help improve the Hinterland Chocolate Company business.

Ah, what a mess. Her heart said get the hell out of here, her mind said, stick it out, do what you agreed, learn as much as possible. And then there was Jamie. Once, she would have done anything for him, even given her life for him. But now?

Jamie stood in front of her. She had always been in his shadow. At six foot, he was tall—tall enough for a man—and while she was short, and like old times, she found herself gazing up at him. She closed her mouth and hoped that she had successfully removed any adoration from her eyes.

'Give it two weeks. Stick around for two weeks and we'll do our mentoring thing. If you still can't stand it after that, I'll fly you home.'

'Two weeks?'

'Yep. That's not long. It'll take a week to get over your jet lag. And plus, this is one of the most beautiful places in the world. And you're here, Sapphie. You've travelled across the world alone. Wow. I'm proud of you. I've been told you beat a formidable bunch of applicants.'

Now, he praised her with flattery, saying the right things. 'You promise that if I ask to go home in two weeks, you'll let me?'

'Yes, I promise,' he said, placing his hand on his heart.

It was a stupid sentiment, and she turned away. 'Okay, I'll give it two weeks.'

She snuck a glance over her shoulder. His body sagged with relief and his head nodded. Time stilled. 'Have you eaten?'

Sapphire shook her head. He punched his fingers across the screen of his phone.

'Pizza will be here in fifteen minutes.'

'Pizza, really?'

'It's good . . . but if you'd prefer something else...' Jamie sat in one of two dining table chairs and crossed one leg over the other.

The stance of a battle won?

'Sapphie, how are you? What have you been doing? I can't believe you're still working at Hinterland.'

'Why is that so incredulous? That was our dream; I've fulfilled it.'

He uncrossed his legs. 'Are you married? Do you have children? Tell me everything.'

The guy just kissed her! Was he serious? Did he think this was safer ground? Or that he was entitled to this information? Especially when she knew nothing about him, his new life, or who he'd become. Or . . . the real reason why he had left.

'Seb will be so proud when I tell him it's you heading up this section of Grindelwald. He was so impressed with the company and its chocolates and how successful it is.'

'Seb?' Jamie seemed lost.

'Seb submitted the application on my behalf without telling me. He only revealed what he'd done after I'd won. If "won" is the right word. He was so happy and begged me to accept knowing that my heart wasn't in it. The team were desperate for me to make this trip, to travel, see the world, and continue following my passion for chocolate.' There was no way she would reveal that the true motivation of her work mates was for her to start living again, to do something—anything—with her life after she'd pretty much moped around for the last five years in a mire of misery and lovesickness. The five years since Jamie had left.

His mobile phone pinged, and Jamie strode to the door where a pizza delivery man stood. As he placed the steaming hot box onto the table, she watched him. His familiar movements, his scent in the air—him, everywhere, here. A sob rippled across her chest, and she caught her breath, repressing it but failing. It released as an ugly moan. She covered her mouth as if that would bind her back together and keep her in one piece. Jamie hurried over and put his arms around her.

Did he think he was offering comfort?

Damn him for feeling so good, but nauseating at the same time. With surprising force, she yanked her body out of his grip and forced them apart, Jamie's arms left hanging.

'Thank you for the pizza, but I can't be here with you. Can you—can you, leave?'

Jamie considered her, appearing to weigh up whether to

agree or to insist he'd stay. Reaching a decision, he nodded. The door clicked shut after he'd left, and she was alone.

James coloured the white chocolate with food dye, making it pink because that was Sapphie's favourite colour. When the mixture reached a light rose gold shade, he filled the piping bag and manoeuvred it carefully across the mould, creating perfect thin strips that would pop against the dark chocolate. The colour reminded him of Sapphie's face when she blushed so that her cheeks glowed rosy.

Pausing, he sipped his scotch and listened to the ice chink together as he placed the glass back on the bench. It was a calming sound and a good distraction. Deliberately shaking the stout glass, he made the cubes crash against each other again. After another sip, he took an overly large intake of breath—a reverse sigh.

Seeing Sapphie had wreaked havoc on his mood. He'd switched between surprise, joy and anguish, and now he was simply glum. And very alone. His house was elaborate and large and a showpiece of Austrian architecture, but sometimes, even to him, it appeared ostentatious and overdone, and he felt over-whelmed by the spaciousness and its solitude.

But "glum" was too soft a word to sum up his emotions. His hands and limbs twitched and he needed to do *something*.

Chocolate was always the answer. The kitchen was where he needed to be. He loved his gleaming industrial stainless-steel kitchen and found joy and contentment amongst its rectangular shape, high benchtops, and marble surfaces with modern appliances. Would it work its magic today?

Having already prepared the dark cocoa butter, he sprayed the mould, which would form a lining for the outside of the artisan chocolates. For him, hand-crafting was the only way to make chocolate. Original and individual fine treats were the most authentic of chocolate making.

The layer of cocoa butter was so fine that it dried quickly. His mood escalated with the next step—his favourite part. Tempering was such an important part of the process. Stirring was methodical, gentle, and calculating. It was essential to reach the right temperature to ensure it was easy to work with. During that time, his thoughts centred solely on the chocolate. A drop splattered onto his thumb, and he licked it off, savouring the bitter taste. But then he remembered Sapphie's lips on his, and he shivered and tensed. His hand gripped the spoon, and he stirred too fast. If he pushed any harder, it would go solid and be ruined. He forced himself to calm down.

Problem was that his head wasn't on the task. His brain was filled with thoughts of home, his previous life, and the things from which he'd run. It was like being slapped in the face or waking up alive inside your nightmare. But Sapphie wasn't a nightmare; perhaps home might be.

She looked so good, hardly changed, just like the girl he used to know. But there was an edge to her, something he'd never detected before. Cynicism, distrust, weariness? No, it was bitterness. She had always been the quintessential lovely girl next door—friendly, happy to help anyone, and caring; it was hard to find fault with her. Well, he guessed, the fault was that she was always too good, too perfect.

Unlike him.

She'd always been ethereal and delicate as if she belonged in a different world. That hadn't changed, despite the hardness to her soft edges; it only made her more alluring. Even after all this time, he was immediately attracted, drawn to her, just as he always had been. Her smile could brighten up a room and those eyes always reminded him of a salty olive, that dull off-green camouflage colour appearing even duller when she was sad, yet sparkling to a more emerald shade in the sun.

It was difficult to be with someone so perfect, someone everyone adored, someone people trusted, particularly when he wasn't the same. But that wasn't why he had left. He'd spent a long time getting the memory of home out of his head and would be damned if he was going to let it back in now.

The moonlight illuminated his kitchen, casting an eerie glow that suited his mood perfectly. No other lights brightened up the house, and shadows danced on the walls. Soft, mellow jazz music played, and James tapped his foot to the rhythm.

Sapphire Banks. Damn it! He couldn't stop thinking about her and still couldn't believe she was here, rocking his world in all sorts of ways. James closed his eyes and recalled the feel of her against him—like old times. She had responded to his touch, too.

What did that mean?

He would be lying to say he never thought of her. He tried his best not to; any recollection brought up painful memories, thoughts he couldn't control, events he couldn't rewind.

With a calmer movement now, he saturated the mould with the milk chocolate at the perfect temperature. The liquid dripped over the edges, spreading across the marble bench. With precision, he whipped out his spatula and shaved the excess from the top, adding to the mess but not caring. Shaking the mould, he worked it to remove any bubbles. Once smooth, he tipped the excess out, leaving perfectly covered and shaped moulds, and placed the tray to the side.

Standing stock still with his feet shoulder-width apart for balance, he used the spatula to scoop, mould, and play with the globs of chocolate covering the surface in front of him. So much goodness! He dipped a finger in and let it linger in his mouth, imagining he was licking the liquid off Sapphire's body.

Argh!

He wanted to scream. Stop thinking about her. He smoothed the mixture into a rectangle to let it set into a slab of wafer-thin chocolate.

James had done a pretty good job of moving on. He'd created another life for himself—one that didn't involve home, or his father, or Hinterland Chocolate. The collateral damage had been Sapphire. What was his father doing now? James pictured him drunk in his wheelchair, yelling belligerently at some football game on the television. They'd shared a passion for sport, but not much else and certainly not for each other.

Then, of course, there was Seb—his old employer who'd given him a chance, taught him what he knew, and how to be a great chocolatier. Sapphire said she was fulfilling their dream. He'd dreamed a lot since he'd left, but not of that shattered hope, nor of the future he'd thought they'd have together; Sapphire and living in Australia, probably being the best choco-latiers on home soil.

His stomach went cold, and his demeanour hardened, turning him to stone and making the scotch chill. This was how he'd coped, freezing himself out, out of a past he didn't want to remember, forcing himself to forget and hardening his heart in the process.

And now Sapphire was here. What were the chances, huh? Of the thousands of applicants, she was the chosen one. Pouring another scotch, straight up this time, he downed it in one gulp. Yeah, that warmed him, so he downed another.

Mixing hazelnut paste with more milk chocolate and cocoa butter, he made the filling. He nurtured the mixture, taking extra care. The meditative movement pleased him, and he stirred for longer than necessary, but once satisfied, he retrieved another piping bag from his collection and, with delicate care, filled each shell, slowly and one at a time. These moulds were shaped like a perfectly round moon. Once filled, he placed the tray into the cooling cabinet.

The music hit a crescendo and James slammed the cabinet door, so hard it flung back and almost struck him in the face. His drink was empty and he reached for another to slice the edge off his mood and release his hunched shoulders.

Waiting for the mould to cool only allowed more memories to surface, flooding his mind. Yanking out the tray earlier than he should, he warmed the already prepared chocolate and added the last layer. The thick, dark mixture oozed over the top. He capped the tray and scraped off the excess. It had to cool again to set, so he plonked himself onto the bench and used his fingers to pick at the hardening slab. Cracking it, he relished the sound; the sign of good chocolate is the "snap". He kept snapping like a madman, until the entire slab was a desecrated mess of odd pieces. James ate one, then another. Closing his eyes, he savoured the taste on his tongue, swirling it around. He would never ever get sick of chocolate. It had been both his downfall and his saviour.

Was Sapphire a good chocolatier? She couldn't be marvellous because why else would Seb send her across the world to learn from someone else? Granted it was someone they didn't think was him. And why had the company been so desperate for her to come?

He sat bolt upright, his hand landing in the mound of chocolate, instantly melting it into a mushy mess. Lifting his fingers to his mouth, his tongue rolled along the skin of each knuckle, tasting the chocolate and devouring it until his hands were clean. It clung to the corners of his lips, and a drop escaped dribbling down his chin.

She'd said Seb wasn't aware he was the illustrious expert chocolatier, so the company hadn't sent her to get answers or worse, retribution. He swirled his fingers once more through the melting chocolate pooling on the bench. He zig-zagged them one way, then another. Dark milk chocolate splashed against his white shirt, staining it brown. The exquisite liquid ran through his fingers and down his arms. He didn't stop until long, spidery strips spilled over the edges and down his cabinets. He'd made one hell of a mess.

Thoughts of home were driving him crazy. This wasn't a conspiracy theory; no one had done anything malicious. It was simply a ridiculous scenario. Of course, no one at home knew the truth. He'd been gone for more than five years, no one knew what had happened back then.

Well, at least he hoped so.

Chapter Six

'Oh my gawd, it's so beautiful,' Daisy shouted as Sapphire scanned the market square with her phone. 'It's like a toy village!'

'Sure is,' Sapphire replied. 'But show me Winston again.' Her sister placed the phone close to her beloved dog's face. His tiny pink tongue lashed out smudging the screen. Sapphire sucked in a deep breath. Seeing him, hearing his barks and whimpers, talking to home, it was both cathartic and heartbreaking simultaneously. Over the past five years, she'd rarely been parted from him.

Yep, she needed to get a life. In her short, twenty-eight years she'd failed miserably so far.

'Is that pastry on your lips?' her eldest sister, Olive, asked.

'Um, yes, and it was delicious.' She giggled and wiped the back of her hand across her mouth.

'I thought you were in Austria, not France,' her mother queried. Her entire family was squashed into the tiny rectangle shape of her phone screen. They sat as a clumped group that smiled down the camera.

'I think it's the German version of pastry.' She leaned closer to the phone. 'And not nearly as good as an almond croissant.'

'Is the coffee okay?' her dad asked. They were hitting her with the hard questions. He held Winston in his arms as he wriggled, and her heart performed a funny little jig in her chest. Watching him, she was slow to respond, and the faces of her family stared at her, expectant. 'Um, yes, it's good—strong.'

But she'd talk about food and coffee all day. Her lips were sealed on Jamie. She wasn't yet ready to share that fact, or even utter those words out loud, particularly when she wasn't sure of the response she'd receive. Her family might be outraged, demand her return, and want to speak to him. They'd have her back for sure, but she wanted, needed to process this disaster for herself first. And if she was honest, she didn't want to be persuaded that she should return home pronto.

Punching end call, a flash of whimsy overcame her. The urge to receive a squishy cuddle from her dog was overwhelming. Dreaming of a cuddle with her dog? She really did need to get a life.

It was Saturday morning in Hallstatt and she sat in the village square, the heart of the town where it buzzed with activity. Small in size, it sure packed a punch with cafés, restaurants and shops decorated in muted tangerines, blues, pinks and creams. Plus, those triangular-shaped rooves. Why didn't we design our houses like this? It was so beautiful and distinct, but perhaps it would become nauseating after a while. The café where she sat had timber tables out its front and flower boxes lining its windows. Already, that was her favourite part of this place. The burst of flowering blossoms against the backdrop of the coloured buildings and solid timbers was striking.

A trickle of water sloshed down the Holy Trinity Foundation in the middle of the square. The tourist brochures scattered in front of her revealed its name. People lounged on the steps leading up to it and the concrete barrier surrounding it. The sun was shining, not too hot making it a perfect spot to sit.

'Sapphire?'

She turned towards the voice. 'Hi, Lina.'

'Good morning. Great to see you out and about enjoying our picturesque town and the glorious weather.' She smiled so wide and talked so animatedly, immediately raising Sapphire's spirits. 'How are you feeling after yesterday?'

What? How did she know? Sapphire stumbled over her words. 'What do you mean?'

Lina laughed, an elegant, attractive sound, just like how she looked. Today, her long, wavy blonde hair was pulled back into a stylish high ponytail. She paired it with slim leg jeans and stiletto heels that added to her already impressive height. Despite it being Saturday, she wore red lipstick that complemented the red suede of her shoes. Sapphire loved those shoes! She'd never be brave enough to wear them; surely, they must hurt one's toes with those pointed ends?

'I mean after the first segment yesterday with James. I thought it went well.'

Sapphire sat back in her chair and smiled. 'Yes, I think it went well, too. It was overwhelming being filmed, but you know...' She shrugged. 'Will all of our time together be recorded?'

'Ah, nah. But never say never.' Lina paused and looked around her. 'So, I'll see you at the party?'

Sapphire took another sip of her coffee and coughed, covering her mouth. 'I don't know anything about a party.'

Lina looked aghast. 'What? I'm so sorry. It's a staff party, a thank you from the company but also a welcome for you. It's an opportunity for you to meet everyone.' She rummaged around in her oversized leather handbag and pulled out a scrap of paper. 'Here, these are the details. You can walk from your accommodation; it's not far. You'll come, yes?'

Sapphire hesitated. Geez, she wasn't even a party person at home, let alone here. Jet lag still licked at her heels, and her head could go from clear to foggy in a second. She had to buy groceries for the week ahead and needed to get the lay of the land. She read the note in her hand. 'It's at James' house?' she asked, swallowing the lump that had formed in her throat.

'*Ja*, he's the boss, and he's hosting. It's going to be an amazing party. You can't miss it!'

It was too much too soon. She needed to regroup and get her head in order. But more importantly, she wanted to minimise her contact with Jamie. Just as she was about to refuse and feign fatigue, Lina said, 'Fabulous. I'll see you there in a few hours,' and blew her a kiss before she walked away.

At the roar of an elephant, Sapphire jumped a foot off the ground. 'What the bleeding heck?' she mumbled as she walked down the long concrete drive. Raised voices mixed in with background music and a cacophony of animal sounds led her in the right direction. A multi-coloured tent sat on a vast expanse of a perfectly manicured green lawn. Was it a fancy marquee, Austrian style?

But no, it was a circus tent resplendent with a big top and clowns circling, some on unicycles, while others wandered around juggling, wearing the distinctive white faces with painted-on large red grins. A pen of animals was to the side, with hay stacked around the edges, where some brave people offered sticks to the elephants, but understandably, not to the lions held securely, she hoped, in cages. Women rode horses bareback, wearing a variety of garishly bright costumes.

Sapphire rubbed her eyes, thinking she had to be dreaming. But no, when she opened them, the circus tent and animals remained.

What the...?

Turning in the other direction, the house came into view. Something out of a Disney fairy-tale, it was a multi-storied, yellow-toned building with brown trims, brick chimneys, and gabled balconies on each level but no flower boxes. To add to the effect, lush gardens surrounded it making it picture-postcard perfect against a deep royal blue sky. She wanted to rip out her phone and capture it, remember the detail. Jamie lived here? Sapphire shook her head. Who on earth had he had become?

Not recognising anyone gathered, she walked through the crowd and entered a large terrace with a pool. Where was the fence? She was prone to ridiculous, pragmatic thoughts at times and worried that small children, or drunk people might fall into the pool and drown. She'd have to be vigilant.

Wait staff dressed in black and white attire moved through the crowd, offering drinks and nibblies. Or would they be called canapés here? A long banquet table lined one edge of the terrace and displayed a plethora of food. Tables of fruit piled high, whole wheels of cheese with large wedges removed sat with crackers and antipasti, olives, and bread sticks. Pretty much anything your heart desired was available. Sapphire stole one solitary grape and popped it in her mouth. Pathetic, with all of this food on offer, she took a grape...

Along the adjoining edge was a string quartet. As she spun the other way, she spied a band of the more traditional rock style playing, replicating a rock concert where people danced on the grass in a mosh-style pit.

Her head spun, so when the next waiter offered her a glass of champagne, she took it and sipped once, then twice. The icy cold liquid fizzed up her nose but tasted like no sparkling wine she'd drunk before. Light and fruity, it went straight to her head.

'Sapphire!' Marcus pulled her into an embrace. Sapphire sagged with relief at the familiar face. He clinked glasses and shouted, '*Salute*!' before gulping his drink. 'It's going to be a great afternoon,' he declared, keeping his arm around her middle. 'What a party!' He twirled her on the spot in his excitement. 'Let me introduce you to everyone.'

Marcus proceeded to drag her by the arm and introduced her to the remainder of the PR team, which she summed up as small but dynamic.

'But, Marcus,' she said as they by-passed large groups of people, 'who are these people?'

'Oh, they work in the factory on the production lines making the chocolates.' He didn't pause, dragging her along until they ran into Lina.

'Sapphire!' Lina squealed acting as if she hadn't seen her

only hours before. Lina pulled her into a hug, holding too tight for too long. Was this the Austrian way? The French kissed your cheeks; perhaps the Austrians were touchy-feely? To Sapphire, it felt a bit staged and overly familiar.

'Have you met everybody?' Lina asked. Preparing to say no, Marcus jumped in to confirm she had and retrieved three further drinks from the nearest tray.

Everyone was in an exultant mood. The circus performers wore broad grins matched by the guests. People laughed, drank, ate and danced. Sapphire had to agree that she'd never seen anything like it, though she hardly went to parties anyway. Perhaps it was a European thing to hire entertainment and staff?

A microphone crackled to life, and the crowd turned expectantly to the staircase that descended to the terrace area. Jamie stood on the top step, waving to get their attention. 'Welcome, and thank you for coming, everyone. To the faithful, loyal and hardworking staff of Grindelwald Hallstatt, this party is for you.' Everyone erupted in cheers and raised their glasses.

Sapphire's adrenaline spiked at the sight of him and she leaned forward, soaking up each word.

'I've only been here in Austria a short time but I wanted to thank you for your hard work, and commitment to the company and our chocolate. Without you, there'd be no chocolate. But today is not about chocolate or work; it's about fun!' More cheers. Lina appeared at Jamie's side and whispered in his ear, and his expression changed from jubilation to serious in an instant. His eyes searched the crowd. 'And of course, today is also to welcome our new mentee all the way from Australia,' he stumbled over the word, 'please welcome Sapphire Banks. She'll be with us for the next three months to learn about our wonderful chocolate.' The crowd tittered and searched for the new recruit amongst them.

Marcus pushed Sapphire in the back, spilling champagne down her front, and raised his hand in her direction. Stepping back, the crowd parted, placing her in the spotlight. Sapphire caught Jamie's gaze. He didn't smile or offer reassurance; he simply repeated her name and pointed to where she stood. Old Jamie would never have allowed her to bear such unwanted attention alone. But just as quickly, he diverted attention away and spoke in broken German to the pleasure of the crowd.

Was that his attempt to rescue her? She didn't know anything anymore.

Like an evangelical preacher, he stood before his followers responding to their jeering and the shouting of his name. Finally stepping down, he shook hands with each man and kissed the cheeks of each woman, seemingly familiar with every guest.

She'd adored him once like that, too. Sapphire looked at her feet and took control of her ragged breathing. Her breathlessness was due to the situation, not him.

Today, he was dressed casually in chinos and trousers that hugged his legs, as well as a collared polo. The sun caught the curls of his hair and turned it a lighter shade of brown. He smiled broadly and kindly and spoke to everyone.

A clown juggling balls appeared in front of her, blocking her view of Jamie. He mimicked her serious demeanour and cajoled her to smile. His silly antics worked, and her grin broke through. Placing the balls into her hands, he attempted to teach her to juggle. The balls tumbled and rolled into the pool. The clown made a sad face, pulled more from his pockets and laughed. He tried again, but Sapphire batted him away, and he found another victim.

Alone now, Sapphire searched for Marcus or Lina. Marcus was across the way, talking to a handsome young man. Perhaps she had him pegged wrong and didn't need to worry about his overly friendly advances? Lina was nowhere in sight. Jamie continued to work the room.

Sapphire headed for the food table and piled her plate with the generous offerings. Noticeably, there wasn't a morsel of chocolate: no chocolate foundation, fondue, or even brownies.

Interesting.

Nibbling on a cracker, she headed for a group of people who were talking quietly at the far end of the terrace. If this worked and they welcomed her, she'd reward herself for her bravado and bravery; if they rejected her, she'd dump her plate and run.

Luckily, they offered warm smiles upon her arrival and chatted with her in broken English.

Marie and Jakob were a married couple who had met at the factory, married and had worked there for most of their adult lives. They held hands and smiled fondly as they spoke. Both loved their jobs and chocolate, and now, they loved the Grindelwald chocolate. Sapphire shook her head in wonderment; you couldn't pay for better loyalty and service. This was also the Hinterland way. She hoped that Jamie would greet Marie and Jakob and thank them personally.

They invited her to visit them on the line, and she'd said she'd loved them to "show her the ropes". They'd laughed at her Australian expression, and she laughed with them and agreed to catch up with them next week.

Wandering away, Sapphire searched for a bathroom.

Heading towards the house, she entered a back door and found it quiet as compared to the frivolity of the party. There were no indications of the toilet's direction so she opened a random door and peeked inside. Her heart raced, and her eyes goggled.

A living area.

Sparsely furnished but tasteful, it featured light gold walls with cream furniture and a glass-topped coffee table. Paintings adorned the walls, adding a pop of colour. Large bay windows flooded the space with light. An antique-style timber bookcase sat at the far end. It was warm and inviting, and nothing like what she'd expected.

At home, all those years ago, Jamie had lived with his disabled dad in a small, nondescript two-storey chamferboard house on the outskirts of Canungra. It had bare floorboards and minimal furniture and lacked personal touches, not a plump cushion, coloured vase or plaid rug.

A noise behind her made her spin around. A waiter arrived with empty glasses. 'I'm sorry,' she said. 'Can you direct me toward the bathroom.' He gestured for her to follow and they walked through the kitchen.

Whoa! A full-scale galley style kitchen with modern stainless-steel appliances, a grey-flecked marble bench top, and splashes of warmth, in the bar stools, in the coloured crockery on display, and quirky framed pictures.

'*Danke,*' she said as he gestured to the room behind the kitchen. A revelation came to Sapphire as she washed her hands at the basin with its gold taps and white porcelain trim. The man she knew and loved, the one she had spent the last five years pining for, was not the man here today. Jamie was a young chocolatier she knew in Australia. That man no longer existed.

James was an entirely different person. He was famous, sophisticated and a wealthy chocolatier of Europe. And he held flamboyant parties with exotic circus animals.

With that realisation came sudden clarity and relief. She could do this; she could be a mentor to someone she didn't know. Moreover, this might be exactly what she needed—the solution to force her to stop longing for a man who no longer existed. She might have loved Jamie, but Jamie was no more. And she didn't love James, so maybe finally, she could move on with her life and forget Jamie. Ironically, James might just be the man to make that happen.

Chapter Seven

'Come in.' James responded to the rap on his office door but didn't look up from his computer screen.

'Morning, boss,' Lina sang out, placing a double espresso keep-cup in front of him. 'I'll grab the paperwork from my office and be back in a minute.'

'Hmm.' James kept working, tapping on the keys until he became aware of a presence. Sapphie sat in the chair in front of his desk. A bolt of pleasure shot through him before he slapped the lid of the laptop shut, and scanned his desk, tidying the stray pieces of paper into piles. 'Good morning,' he said.

'Morning,' she replied, her voice husky.

And then nothing. 'Did you enjoy the party?'

'The party?' she said vaguely as if she'd forgotten about it.

He reclined in his high-back leather chair. He hated being patronised. 'Yes, you know the event on Saturday with the elephants and tigers? I went to a rather lot of effort.'

'Is that how you hold parties over here? It certainly was a lot of rigmarole. But the staff enjoyed your . . . spectacle,' the word rolled off her tongue.

'Hm. Did you . . . enjoy the spectacle then?'

She matched him by lounging back and making herself comfortable in the cushioned armchair. James sensed a shift in her, a confidence, no, a defiance. He controlled his smirk.

'Yes, thank you.' Her words were measured and controlled. 'I met some very nice people from the factory.'

'The factory?' He took a quick sip of his coffee, his eyes darting sideways. 'Look, while we're alone, I wanted us to agree that it's probably best not to mention that we know each other or, you know, the particulars of my past.'

'Your past? You mean us?' She wasn't making this easy.

'Yes, you know, our relationship, home, where we come from. It's not anyone's business, and they don't need to know. There's nothing to gain by bringing up old news...'

Sapphie interrupted. 'You mean all of it? Our relationship, Canungra, working together at the factory, your humble beginnings. Is that what you want to be kept a secret?' Her intonation rose with each word, as she placed one hand on each arm of the chair.

He took a deep breath. 'I guess it sounds strange. But I've worked hard to be in this position, and I don't want there to be any risk of damage...'

'To your reputation?' There she went again.

He hung his head. 'You make it sound terrible. Is it so bad to keep the past in the past?'

'No, but it sounds like you're embarrassed about where you've come from and who you used to be.'

'I'm not who I used to be.' His retort was too fast, too stern. He was making a mess of this.

'Isn't that clear, *James*? Sort of makes things easier. In fact, I agree. Let's agree we don't know each other because the truth is, we don't. It'll be simple and easy. I don't know who you are anymore anyway. You're a stranger.' It was the first sign of fluster.

'Sapphie . . . c'mon, I haven't changed that much.'

'Don't do that. You can't act as if you know me in one breath and call me by nicknames, then direct and dictate what I say and ask that I pretend we don't have a past. Just to be clear you don't want me to refer to our previous relationship or your beginnings at Hinterland Chocolate? Is that right?'

He nodded. 'And don't mention my father.'

Her eyes widened further, but the retort sitting on the tip of her tongue remained unsaid as the door banged open and Lina returned.

'Sorry about that. I forgot the confidentiality agreement.' She placed a document on James' desk which he quickly retrieved. He glanced at Sapphire to catch the roll of her eyes.

Lina volleyed glances between them. When he peeked up, Lina's eyes had narrowed, and her face was scrutinising.

He ignored Lina. 'This is a confidentiality agreement regarding what you see and learn here at Grindelwald. Quite straightforward and procedural.' Handing it over, Sapphire took the document and scanned it quickly while he sipped his coffee.

'I don't get it. I'm here to learn about your skills and techniques in this factory, but I'm forbidden from disclosing what happens here or revealing any of your company secrets. I'm confused. Aren't

I supposed to return home and implement some of these new skills in *my* factory? Isn't that the whole point? So, if I'm using the new knowledge I acquired from here, how do I keep that confidential?'

Lina jumped in and he was grateful. Bloody hell, Sapphire frazzled him, but he didn't frazzle easily. In fact, hadn't been frazzled since he'd left home. He had left behind his whole world and its complications. In his new domain, the one he'd created, he was in complete control and stress was only created when someone else messed up. An aloof and carefree personal life, where he didn't form long-term attachments to anyone, also kept his private life tidy.

But this woman had well and truly frayed his edges since her arrival, and his regulated existence was unravelling.

'It's simple, Sapphire. What this document means is that you aren't to discuss what you learn and see here with our competitors.'

'What's such a big secret? The ingredients to chocolate are pretty standard, as are the processes, so what could I possibly divulge to *your competitors*?'

His guarded composure slipped. 'Let's simplify this. Don't talk to other people about Grindelwald chocolate. Full stop. Don't speak to the press, whether local or at home, or to other chocolatiers or companies. When you return to Australia, you can utilise whatever you've learned here, but simply don't publicise the exact measures you implement or any tricks or tips you've learned.'

'This is ridiculous,' she exclaimed, holding the document up and looking at him, her eyes squinting in disbelief. 'Why go to the trouble of having this program and me, or anyone in this position if we're gagged?'

From the moment she'd sat in his office, he'd experienced more emotions than he typically felt in an entire day. Now, he wanted to reassure her and make her understand, but business was business, and he'd never again go through what he'd experienced before.

'The terms are not negotiable and mandatory. Don't talk to the press. Don't accept payment for sharing information about Grindelwald, whether that means our chocolate or about the factory or even who works here. You aren't permitted to take photographs or document what you see or learn.'

'So pretty much don't talk to anyone ever about Grindel-wald chocolate?'

'Yes.'

Sapphire hung her head low and examined her lap in great detail. Her chest rose and fell with her breaths. He had forgotten how smart she was, how tenacious. Most people underestimated Sapphire because of her quiet demeanour and desire to avoid conflict. They didn't realise how switched on she was. She was a staunch believer in justice, doing the right thing and being honest. And was ever so savvy.

Sapphire fiddled with a bracelet, and his gaze zeroed in on the gold at her wrist. His heart jumped into his throat. The bangle. It was only just visible on her slight wrist, peeking out the end of her long sleeve. Sapphire still wore the bangle he'd given her for their first anniversary. He glanced at her face, but her eyes remained downcast. Faced with the evidence of their past, the lump in his throat magnified and it hurt to swallow; his mouth was suddenly dry.

'I don't know anything about the legalities of the agreement, but I need your assurances that I can use what I learn in the factory back home. Otherwise, it's a waste of time. My being here, this project . . .' Her words faltered as she followed his gaze to her arm. She quickly pushed the bangle up into her sleeve where it could not be seen.

His eyes focused on her once more. 'That is agreed.'

Lina offered her a pen. Sapphire looked at Lina, then at him, took the pen and quickly scribbled her signature before handing the document over. He signed next to her; the same signature she'd always had, the one he knew well. He was doing his job, doing what was necessary; why then did he feel like such a prick, and that perhaps, Sapphie might not forgive him, once again?

***

Sapphire fondled the bangle again through her sleeve. She wouldn't make the mistake of revealing it in Jamie's presence again.

Habit. But oh, her stomach swooped at what he might think. What could she possibly say about the fact that she still wore his gift after all this time? Most scorned girlfriends would have hocked it, burned it, given it away, or at the very least, placed it in the bottom drawer. She would never divulge that she'd pined for him like a lost dog since he had left and the bangle reminded her of the good times.

Her hands trembled, and she clutched them tightly to stop the shaking.

Jamie held open his office door and waited for her to pass. As she moved through the doorway, she paused, and inhaled his sweet yet woody scent. It was a delightful aroma, almost good enough to eat. It was new, too, like everything else about him.

She intended to use that to her advantage. Moving forward in slow motion, their arms brushed, and her eyes widened. They were mere millimetres apart; her skin tingled and she forced one foot in front of the other to create distance. She mustn't get close to Jamie; it wouldn't help her purpose and made her blood pressure spike.

'The first thing I want to do is give you a tour of our facility. You need to be familiar with how we make our chocolate on a large scale.'

Sapphire followed him blindly through the compact office spaces of the company, filled with clear green glass and modern fixtures with deep, warm brown tones and numerous potted plants. The walls were exposed brick, providing texture to the beautiful space. Sapphire couldn't help but compare it to the back den where Seb sat in a tiny cubbyhole of a room with a simple Formica desk and a computer with a filing cabinet behind. Her boss's office was at the rear of the building, near the toilet.

Here, the offices were on the second storey of a building that was located on the outskirts of the village. However, "outskirts" was slightly misleading as everything in Hallstatt was within walking distance.

At the staircase, Jamie arched his arms upwards. 'On top of the building is an open bar and casual space for staff to enjoy their breaks and after-work drinks. I'll show you that later.'

Yes, Hinterland had a similar terraced space out the back door near the exit, with plastic outdoor furniture, usually toppled sideways in the weather, with extra seating available on the concrete retaining wall nearby. The décor didn't matter; it was about the chocolate anyway, and Sapphire could vouch

that Hinterland's products matched their European coun-
terparts.

After descending two sets of stairs, they arrived back in the
reception area which had two large, swing-back doors leading to
the production floor.

'Do you offer tours to tourists? It's quite popular now to get
visitors onto the factory floor.'

'No, never.' Jamie answered quickly. 'This is a working
space, not a tourist attraction. The famous salt mine, you must
visit while you're here, is the biggest attraction in Hallstatt. It
offers tours, but it is no longer operational. This is a workplace.
We don't even have a shop, but there's one in the village square,
very close.' He repeated, 'We are an operational business and our
focus is making the chocolate.'

Okay, message delivered loud and clear. Weird. But okay,
Hinterland didn't offer tours either, but they had a prominent
shop out the front that attracted large volumes of visitors.

Jamie hit a green button and the doors opened automati-
cally as they entered the floor. Immediately, Sapphire relaxed. Of
course, this wasn't her factory, but it was where she loved being,
where she spent most of her time. Entering the sterile, clean
environment with the overwhelming rich, evocative smell was
welcoming, normal, and usual. And yet, excitement swirled in
her tummy.

'Mr White. Telephone call for you, Sir.' A member of staff
appeared to their right, where they whispered together.

'I've got to take this.' Jamie turned away, scanning the
spacious room. 'Emmanuel!' He gestured with his fingers to the
man. 'I'm giving,' he paused, looked at her a moment too long,

'our mentee a tour but I must attend to something. Can you continue?'

Emmanuel readily agreed and offered her a broad smile. He was a large, round man with strands of a bushy beard peeking through a face mask and a thick, strong accent. A local; that made her happy.

Jamie rushed away, filled with importance, and Sapphire washed her hands, donned some gloves and put on a hair net.

The factory room wasn't as large as she had anticipated but she guessed a production line running efficiently could make thousands of chocolates per day. They passed the coating machine where rows of square chunks of Turkish delight moved under the chocolate fountain and came out the other side perfectly coated before continuing on their journey and ending in a large batch ready for packaging.

'Let me show you our infamous stars. They are our signature product.' She followed him, waving weakly to members who might glance up from their stations; it would only take a second for an imperfect shape to slip through.

Emmanuel came to a stop in the next room. Thousands of star-shaped chocolates, large, small, and in between, rotated past on conveyor belts. He snatched one up and examined it. 'You've tried this before, yes?' he asked, hovering the chocolate under his nose.

'Of course. They're an icon.' This made him smile. He waved his hand in front of the belt, indicating she should take one too. They were one variety, but she couldn't decipher which flavour yet. Like a child opening a birthday present, she got one in her fingers and smelled it, turned it this way and that, and finally popped it in her mouth and groaning.

'Yum, salted caramel!' she exclaimed, causing Emmanuel to laugh.

'One of the best,' he agreed. 'See over there,' he pointed across the space,' they move along this belt and eventually get to the section where they are wrapped. Given that we produce many of these signature chocolates, they are machine-wrapped these days with a checking system at the end to ensure only the highest standards.' He gestured for her to follow him slowly as they wandered along the side of the belt.

'Everything is running very smoothly now after the transition,' he said.

'Oh, what do you mean?' she asked.

Emmanuel tried to hide his surprise that she didn't know. 'Before becoming Grindelwald, we were a small, independently owned and local brand of Austrian chocolate. The boss worked hard, but it was difficult to achieve the higher standards of Grindelwald. We needed new and improved machinery and more staff because we produce much more product under this name...'

'What were you called before?'

'We were called Mabels, good old fashioned homemade chocolate. With the takeover, Mr White rebranded us under the Grindelwald conglomerate and we are part of them now.' He continued. 'Big changes in small time. He is committed and loves the chocolate. He kept the workers and employed more local people. And now we make Grindelwald chocolate. Everyone is happy.'

'Did the previous owner stay on for a while?' Sapphire's mind churned back to the old man she had expected to be her mentor.

'*Ja*. He did, but that didn't work. Everything was different. Mr White, he knows what he's doing.'

'Gosh, it all sounds like such a risk. I'm sure it's been a big investment especially with the modernisation of the factory.'

Emmanuel shrugged. 'Mr White, he has spent a lot. But with a successful brand like Grindelwald, you cannot go wrong.'

'Jam—ah, Mr White, he just runs it right, though? There's a head office, sort of like a franchise?'

Emmanuel shook his head as he examined more shapes and flavours in front of him. They were white chocolate stars, and she knew they had a strawberry filling. Her mouth watered.

'Franchise?' He gave her a blank look. 'The head office of the company is in Lucerne, Switzerland. This is what you say—like a branch, a division, one of many. Mr White owns the building and the equipment, but the brand is Grindelwald. He is responsible for the production of this chocolate to the same high quality as the main company, and they are involved in aspects of production and marketing,' he said and continued. 'It is an international company, but the head office is open to tourists, offers tours, has a museum, shop, everything. Very popular.'

Sapphire stalled.

Holy shit.

Jamie owned the factory. He hadn't mentioned this rather large detail. Scanning the space again, her eyes boggled. The cost! And no mistaking it, this was a serious operation.

But why was she surprised? Of course, Jamie, no, *James* owned the factory.

They paused in front of a piece of equipment she hadn't seen before, and she asked Emmanuel to explain.

Their heads were bent over its inner workings when Jamie

returned. He slapped Emmanuel on the back, receiving a broad grin in return. The two were close. Emmanuel was clearly a trusted worker, loyal and committed. He bowed his head to Sapphire in thanks and departed, humming as he walked back to his station.

Sapphire tried to retain everything Emmanuel had told her. She fingered the tiny spiral-bound notebook in her pocket, hoping to write it down later. Be damned if any confidentiality agreement was going to stop her.

'Let's head to the kitchen, and we can make some chocolate.'

Thank goodness. Her fingers were itching to get her hands on some tools and get to work.

Chapter Eight

'This is not a real kitchen, is it?' she asked as they entered the same kitchen space they had worked in previously. Jamie laughed. The sound was like a trickling waterfall cascading against rocks.

'Yes, it's a real kitchen but it is designed for demonstrations and since we've started the YouTube channel, for filming segments, ads, etcetera.'

A range of staff hovered around the benches setting out bowls and ingredients. They scurried away like frightened mice as the pair approached.

'There you are,' Lina exclaimed as she entered the room with her usual crew. The cameraman, the hair and make-up lady, and one other person Sapphire didn't know. Lina's PA, maybe, because she always had a pen in her hand. No Marcus today. Lina barked orders and they hurried to set up. Sapphire's heart sank. They were being filmed again? She was becoming an actress playing a part rather than a student trying to learn the craft. But, then again, that was exactly what she was doing, right? Acting.

Standing at the bench, she observed the set-up. 'Why don't we arrange our own ingredients? Don't you think it's important to ensure the amounts are exact and the quality is perfect?'

James stood next to her, too close. His chest rose and fell.

'The ingredients aren't a secret...' but as she uttered the words, she realised it was true.

'Of course not,' he exclaimed, but she didn't believe him. He stood stiff and uncomfortable.

'That's absurd. I can name the ingredients,' and she said them out loud, her voice slightly too high. The crew stopped and stared and the camera guy moved into position. He was curtly pushed away by Jamie and scuttled to the rear of the room. Jamie's hand was on hers, and she stopped prattling but immediately pulled it away.

'Are you ready?' Lina.

Bright white light illuminated where they stood, and both protected their eyes. The rest of the room dimmed. Jamie inhaled deeply, seemed to hold it for at least the count of three, then released a big breath with his head bowed. To anyone else, the gesture would not have been discernible. To her, it was obvious—a sign of what?

Frustration? He was frustrated! Hmm, Sapphire observed the room.

Within seconds, Jamie lifted his head. 'We're not doing this today. Lina let's get a couple of still shots, wherever you like. You can post those, do a few reels or whatever, but we're not going to film the lesson today.' He avoided Lina's gaze as it slipped between Sapphire and him and back. Sapphire moved a step back, trying to become invisible.

For a moment, she suspected there might be a stand-off, but Lina simply nodded and manoeuvred them politely into position. The blazing lights were dimmed, and the room returned to normal. Following Jamie's lead, she donned her chef gear, and they stood robotically at the kitchen bench, side by side. Lina threw one of those looks in their direction again and, without words, shuffled them together until their bodies touched. Jamie stiffened. Lina shoved a wooden spoon into his hand, and he grimaced. No tools for her; Lina moved her left hand onto her hip.

It was over in a matter of seconds, but Sapphire held her breath the entire time. She could breathe again when the expensive and ridiculously large camera performed its last click. Then she scooted as quickly as possible to the other end of the bench; Jamie did the same.

'Okay. I'll leave you to it,' Lina addressed Jamie with another pointed stare, which he ignored. Upon her exit, he slammed the door shut and locked it. He fiddled with his phone, and slow, soulful music filled the room. He lit standing lamps in each corner and left only a string of overhead lights illuminated above their workspace.

'The right atmosphere is important for making the chocolate, don't you agree?'

O-k-a-y, she drew the syllables out in her head. Not mood-setting for her, but that was good; she ignored the tinge of disappointment.

Instead of focusing on him, she focused on the bench. She picked up the closest dish and examined the contents, wet her pinkie finger, and tasted. 'Oh my, are these rose petals?'

His eyes twinkled, and he threw her a broad grin. She loved that he responded to her enthusiasm. 'Yes, crystallised pink and red petals. We are going to make our handcrafted white chocolate and pistachio and rose block.' He held up the finished product, a block of about ninety grams, she guessed.

'And these blocks are hand-made, not produced en masse by the machines?' He looked up before answering, checking her expression. Did he think she was having a dig at him?

'Yes, these are the hand-crafted range. Exclusive.' Jamie shifted through a pile on the right and demonstrated the different flavours available.

'Who makes the hand-crafted chocolate? I haven't seen anyone in the factory making them?'

'I do.'

'You make the handcrafted and artisan chocolates by yourself? That's thousands of chocolates. You can't, surely?'

'There was another chocolatier when I arrived, but he objected to the takeover from the local owner to someone he observed to be a flashy foreigner. There was, how should I say, a period of settling in. That man didn't like the changes I made, including transforming the brand to Grindelwald. So, he stayed a while but left about a month ago. It's for the best, but that leaves me...'

Sapphire absorbed this information, and then realisation clicked. 'Did you scheme up this entire mentor thing to recruit a new chocolatier?' She didn't let him finish. 'You said you wanted the best, someone with potential. You wanted to skill the mentee up and recruit them?'

'Don't be ridiculous.'

'But you're not denying it, so I'm right.'

'I've told you the whole idea was for marketing purposes. When we came up with the strategy, the other fellow was still employed.'

'Yes, but it evolved into recruitment, didn't it?'

'The prospect crossed my mind.'

'I'm sorry. I'm sorry I've completely ruined your marketing campaign and recruitment drive.'

There wasn't much to say to that, so they carried on and worked companionably until she broke the silence. 'It must appear as if the role of chocolatier is so simple, don't you think?' He murmured in concentration. 'I mean, if you have good quality ingredients and mix them together into a slab and let it set, well, then you have delicious chocolate.'

He poured his mixture into the square moulds. 'Yes, but that's where most people go wrong. They do not choose the best quality or the right ingredients. And chocolate is so much about temperature and getting that right.'

He'd finished speaking, and she still looked at his lips. She could listen to him speak all day. Instead, she looked away and started tidying. She'd already finished. Had she gone too fast? Done something wrong? Jamie continued to work.

'Why don't you try something else?' he suggested.

She looked behind her, uncertain. Was he saying she could collect other ingredients without his supervision and authorisation? She didn't need to be told twice.

It was time for experimenting and learning and she gathered a range of flavours and textures that she hadn't combined before.

Lost in her own world, Sapphire didn't notice when the music stopped and the room fell still. Jamie stood on the opposite side of the bench, arms crossed, watching.

Shit. 'I'm so sorry, I got carried away. Was I not supposed to use these ingredients? Or this dish? I'll clean up this mess, I promise.'

'You're incredible.' His voice was odd. Low and deep, it made her insides go instantly gooey like the chocolate she worked with. It reminded her of his after-sex voice.

She chanced a glance up. His body was silhouetted in the dimness of the room, a ray of light appearing above his head like a halo. His already dark eyes were moody like a midnight sea. Sapphire swallowed; all the moisture gone from her mouth.

'What, what do you mean?'

'I'm not sure we've picked the right candidate.'

What? 'Yeah, well, we've pretty much established that.' Her words dripped with sarcasm.

'This project was supposed to teach an aspiring chocolatier, take them from ordinary to great. Sapphie, you are already great.'

'Oh, don't be silly.' She shifted on her feet. 'We were both taught by Seb. You've learned a lot more than me since you've travelled overseas and learned from the best. Now you're the best.'

It was as if she hadn't spoken. 'It was always the case. I'd forgotten. You learned more quickly, picked up things so fast, and had natural talent. Yes, I'm talented and expertly qualified teachers have taught me, but you've got it. In here,' he said, pointing to his chest.

Her heart raced so fast now that it felt like it was hammering outside her chest. He reached across the small space and clasped her fingers in his. 'I'm so sorry,' he choked on the words. 'I'm so sorry for hurting you. For leaving like I did.'

Sapphire had waited a long time for this discussion, and now that it had arrived, the words she'd rehearsed a hundred times were stuck in her throat. Waiting for more, he didn't offer anything else. Wasn't this where he said he was wrong, had made a big mistake and that he still loved her?

He released her fingers and closed the gap between them. He tossed aside her white chef hat, and it landed silently on the floor. He cupped her cheeks with both of his large, muscular hands—hands that had always made her feel safe and wanted and desired. He stared into her eyes, deep down into her soul, before lowering his lips to hers and crushing them, smothering them too hard, too fast—a clash of teeth that delivered a tsunami of emotion with his touch. She was hungry for him, and the tease of his tongue caressing the inside of her mouth sent shivers of desire racing through her. His hands explored her neck and back before resting on her bottom while his lips found her throat, grazing down dangerously close to the dip in her chest.

'I've missed you,' she whispered.

His hands stilled. His lips rose from her collarbone, leaving her skin achingly cold where it had been warm. His forehead leaned against hers as he caught his breath until he removed his hands and stepped away.

His head shook. Her stomach spiralled with fear. No, she

wanted to scream. No. No. No. Her chest already ached, and her arms felt bereft from his absence.

'Shit, Sapphie, I can't help myself around you. But I can't . . . I'm sorry. This is wrong . . .' He avoided her gaze, hands in his back pockets. Sapphire balled her fists. Jamie was hurting her all over again. And she'd let it happen. And after she'd agreed to freeze him out, to pretend they didn't know each other.

And then Jamie fled, just like he'd done all those years ago.

Chapter Nine

Sapphire wrote in her notebook even as the ink on the words of the paper-thin sheet ran. She wanted to document everything after the session before she forgot.

The chocolate she'd made had cooled and set. It was probably still too warm, but she tasted a morsel. Her tongue zinged, and she savoured the dark, roasted chocolate. She had never made chocolate with lemon myrtle before, and it had a distinctive tang. It was sour and sweet all at once and reminded her of the sharp, sugary scent of a morning bakery filled with a variety of delicious treats. With her pen positioned to her lip, she remembered something else and scribbled furiously again, recording amounts and apportionments.

The door flung open, and she jolted at the noise before slapping her book shut and shoving it in her pocket.

'Oh, Sapphire, I thought you were finished your lesson.' Lina moved closer. 'What's wrong?'

She forced a weak smile as the woman placed a comforting arm across her shoulders. 'Nothing, I'm fine.'

'No, you aren't. Was James mean? He can be quite terse when he's stressed.'

'No, not at all . . .'

'I must say, you two are quite strange together. There's an electric chemistry between you; it sizzles in the air when you're in the same room.' She stood over Sapphire with a commanding stance, matched by a tone that indicated she had already reached her own conclusion on the matter. Sapphire's eyebrows rose toward her forehead but perhaps in surprise at being detected rather than in denial. Lina laughed. 'There is something, isn't there?'

Sapphire had agreed not to say anything. But she hadn't spoken to her family, and she was here alone, with no one to talk to. The emotion built up inside her until she felt like she might burst. She could trust Lina; she was one of James' most treasured staff.

She blew her nose before saying, 'We know each other from home.'

Lina grinned; triumphant she'd been right.

'We trained together as chocolatiers and...'

'You were together once?'

Sapphire nodded.

'You loved him?'

The burning desire to talk to someone made the words bubble out of her.

Lina grasped her hand. Her nails were painted gleaming pink, her fingers long and lean. 'I think you're still mourning the relationship you had together. I mean, it's obvious everything is different now. And that was a long time ago...'

Wow. Okay. Was it? Well, yes, she had to agree, but that didn't mean her feelings towards him had diminished. Or that the realisation that he was someone different made it any easier. But she didn't say that.

'Let's have a drink tonight. You can drown your sorrows and have some fun here in Hallstatt. There's a funky little bar I can show you.'

It was tempting, but she shook her head. 'No, thank you, that's very kind. But I'm exhausted and just want to head back to the cabin and get some rest.'

Lina patted her on the arm in a motherly fashion and went to leave.

'Oh, Lina. Is this space usually free? Can I use it when I don't have any sessions with Jam . . . James?'

'Yes, of course. It's all yours. I'll see you tomorrow,' she said, waving as she left.

Sapphire tidied up, removed her apron and hung it with care, placed the chocolate in the cooling room, turned off the lights and ventured outside. It was still daylight, yet the air was cool. The summer months in these countries, with their late sunsets, were divine. So many hours in each day. Unlike her home state which still didn't agree with implementing the concept of daylight saving.

Wandering down streets and alleyways she hadn't discovered before, Sapphire took her time marvelling at the tourists relaxing at the roadside cafes and restaurants, cyclists riding around the lake, and couples wandering hand in hand with a loved one. Home came to mind. What were her family doing? Were they giving Winston lots of cuddles? She hoped Hinterland Chocolate was prospering with many sales; school holidays were always a boost. Extracting her phone, she gazed at the photos of her sisters smiling broadly, hugging her Mum and Dad and then, Winston, of course. She caressed the screen, imagining his pink tongue licking along her chin in greeting and his soft fur against her hands as she rubbed his belly.

All roads in Hallstatt led to the square, and without noticing, she found herself there once more. As she traversed it, she spotted the chocolate shop Jamie had mentioned. Pausing at the window display, she drank in the array of colours, the slabs of marble chocolate and the glass jars. Children's eyes must light up at the possibilities. Her taste buds were tingling at the variety on offer.

As she entered, a bell above the door jangled, and she was immediately greeted with a cheery Austrian hello from the depths of the delightful store. In front of her were trays upon trays of chocolate in every flavour a person could desire. With all of the options, even her mind boggled. Of course, the artisan chocolates made her think of Jamie, and she was staggered once more that he produced these alone. It was phenomenal. She signalled to the lady that she'd like to purchase one of their most enormous boxes and carefully chose a selection of each. She'd play one of her favourite games tonight. When she was small, her mother would buy a collection of chocolates; back then, they were small bite-size bars of different varieties, not these gourmet petite selections. Sapphire would unwrap them and then, with eyes closed, devour them, guessing the flavours. Tonight, she'd do the same. Eat each chocolate, name the ingredients, and note them down in her notebook. She couldn't wait. For the first time today, she had a spring in her step as she left the store.

On the way to the cabin, she purchased a bunch of post-cards featuring the prettiest scenes of Hallstatt. She wouldn't call home and bring on the melancholy it always evoked; she'd write exaggerating what an incredible time she was having. And avoid any mention of Jamie.

Chapter Ten

'**M**arie, Jakob!' Sapphire shouted across the foyer of Grindelwald as she rushed to catch up with them. Marie pulled her into an embrace, and Jakob smiled warmly. 'Nice to see you again.'

'And you, my love. How is your training progressing?'

'Good. No, it's been great; I'm learning lots and enjoying myself.' Saying the words out loud, Sapphire realised it was true, enjoying working on the chocolate anyway.

'What do you have on today?' Marie asked.

Sapphire shrugged and looked around her as if a schedule would jump out at her. 'I'm not sure exactly. Is this morning a good time to come and see where you work?'

'Yes, of course.' The trio wandered into the cavern of the deeper factory, moving into the staff quarters where lockers were lined up against one wall, and people lounged in couches and sat at long benches at a table. It was like a cafeteria. 'Everyone remembers Saphir?' Jakob announced. The small group responded with waves and cheery greetings. She recognised many of the faces and smiled in return.

'Jakob, what did you call me?' she quizzed him.

'Saphir is the translation of your name Sapphire in Austrian.'

'Such a beautiful name,' Marie jumped in.

'So, I pronounced it how we do.'

'I like it,' Sapphire agreed.

An alarm sounded, and staff donned their aprons and hair nets and moved towards an old-fashioned time-punching clock. Sapphire didn't even know what they were called; she'd only seen them in the movies. The staff cordially lined up one behind the other and, once reaching the machine, placed a piece of cardboard underneath in a slot until it punched the time, and then they placed it into a compartment on the wall. Once Marie and Jakob were clocked in, they waved her over but kissed each other goodbye as they were in different parts of the factory today. Jakob was panning, and he explained kindly that he was supervising the coating of the nuts and dried fruits. Sapphire didn't reveal she knew precisely what panning was! She followed Marie, who was on the section that cut, scooped up, and packaged the slabs from the bench after they were set. Stretches of flat chocolate lay before them.

'Yum, honeycomb,' Sapphire murmured as she quietly took place beside the woman and watched her performing her task. 'What's your absolute favourite?' she asked Marie.

The woman laughed. 'That's like asking me, my favourite child. After all these years, I still love chocolate and eat a piece every day, but if I had to pick, I'd say Turkish delight.'

Sapphire made a face, poking out her tongue.

'Okay, your turn. If you could only eat one sort of chocolate ever again, what would it be?'

'Oh, tricky! But I'd say white chocolate with raspberries. It's the best!'

'So, the chocolatier has a sweet tooth.'

'Of course.' They worked silently for a few more minutes. 'You mentioned children, Marie, do they work here?'

Shaking her head, she kept working as she spoke. 'One did initially. But young people have dreams and ambitions, and, often, what is in front of them is too easy, too expected. They dream of something different and yearn for other things. Did you grow up with a chocolate-making family?'

'No. And I sort of fell into it. Now I can't imagine doing anything else.' Would her children follow in her footsteps one day? Who knew?

'Tell me about your Australian family.' Marie asked.

A warmth spread across Sapphire's chest at the thought of her loved ones. 'We live in a small rural town. My father is the local bank manager, and my mother operates luxury cabins on our property. She rents them out to couples for romantic weekends. They are warm and cosy, with glorious views over rolling, green hills and inside they have romantic touches like a fancy spa bath made for two, rose petals, and chocolate, of course!'

Marie was smiling as she stacked. 'Siblings?'

Sapphire nodded. 'Yes, two sisters, Olive and Daisy, I'm the youngest. We're close.' Her voice quivered. 'Olive had childhood cancer, and we were frightened we'd lose her, but she's come through and is cancer-free for now.'

'Oh, that is lovely. It sounds like a nice family.'

Marie went on to describe her son and daughter. Her son

was a teacher, and her daughter was studying medicine. Sapphire heard the pride in her voice and the tenderness in the way she talked. Both had moved away to larger cities with greater opportunities.

The morning flew by, and Sapphire spent the entire time on the line with Marie. They'd chatted through the methodical task. There was a signal for morning tea, and Marie removed her rubber gloves. 'Will you join us in the staff room for a cup of tea?'

'No, thank you, Marie. I'd better go and check if I'm supposed to be anywhere else. Someone might be looking for me.' Somehow, she doubted it, but it was best she check. Despite the circumstances she found herself in, she didn't want to take advantage of the hospitality she was being offered. She might be across the world being challenged in a thousand different ways each day, but she was still that polite girl from Australia. 'Thank you for spending the morning with me.' The two women hugged.

Sapphire made her way back to the entrance and strode up the stairs. The offices were full of people working, but after walking around and peeking into the rooms, she saw no sign of James or Lina. She wandered back down and headed for the kitchen. Inside, she illuminated it as bright as the lights would allow. The pantry was once again stocked with every ingredient one could ever need. She helped herself to the reserves and boiled some milk and chocolate to make a piping cup of hot chocolate. Hot chocolate made with the real stuff was to die for. Once you had drunk it this way, you could never go back to the store-bought variety.

Sipping the delicious, rich liquid, her mind raced with ideas.

She had so much time to fill, but what would she do? Furtively, she glanced around again as if she expected someone to jump out and forbid her to be in the private kitchen space. All remained quiet.

After taste-testing millions of chocolates last night, she was confident she could list the ingredients in most of the artisan slab blocks of chocolate. Yesterday, they made the white chocolate with crystalised rose, but the rest of the range was exquisite. Extracting her notebook, she slid her finger down the page, decided on the recipe she'd tackle, and commenced work.

'Sapphire, here you are. I've been looking for you.'

Her breath hitched at the sound of James' silky-smooth voice. Would there ever be a time she didn't react to him?

Blowing her fringe out of her eyes, she paused a moment before speaking. 'Sorry. Did you need me? I've been here most of the day except for when I was helping Marie on the line.'

Jamie didn't reply. He quickly scanned around her, his eyes narrowing. 'You've made these?' His arms spanned the space. Tray after tray of their artisan chocolate blocks lined the bench space behind her and to her right. She wiped away the last remnants of her chocolate-making efforts from the granite top and rinsed the cloth.

'Yes.'

He stood with his back to her and picked up one of the rectangular pieces of pecan and orange. James performed the usual inspection, and then she heard the snap. It was perfect, and she couldn't help but grin. He nibbled a morsel and then spun to face her.

'Where did you get the recipes?' Without letting her answer, he continued. 'You remember that there is a strict confidentiality agreement, and you can't source the recipes without my permission. They are protected. Who gave them to you?'

She made him sweat for a minute. 'I do not have your secret recipes. I tried each variety last night and worked out the ingredients. I made them from memory and intuition. I'm sure they won't be exactly the same as your usual measurements, but what do you think? Are they good?'

He relaxed then, leaned against the bench, and shook his head. 'Sapphire, are you telling me you made these based on a hunch? You're kidding, right?'

'Nope. Not kidding. And it wasn't hard.'

He sauntered with a sizzling gait along the side of the benchtop and paused to crack in half one example of each she'd made. 'They are perfect,' he said, 'except maybe not that one. Too much coconut.' But he grinned at her as he spoke.

Warmth soared through her body, and she flushed, tugging at the apron crawling too high on her chest. Damn her body for betraying her once more. 'Can you sell them? Are they good enough?'

'Sell them?' He stared at her as if he didn't comprehend.

'You told me you supplied the artisan chocolates. That's a tough gig for one man, even you. If these are good enough, it will help you out. Take the pressure off, you know.' A pause. 'And I can make more.'

'You made these for me?'

Well, she wouldn't quite put it like that, but . . . as his eyes penetrated hers, her skin erupted in goosebumps, and she had to look away.

The distance between them was small, but the gulf felt great. The air crackled but was more like the splitting of the sky before the thunder cracked, heavy, ominous and loaded. He glanced up and broke the silence. 'Thank you. It's perfect. Better than mine.' His face turned away, but she caught the twitch in his eye before he shifted.

Jamie said the right things, but his body language was stiff, and his demeanour was sombre rather than pleasing. Was she wrong to help? But when he turned back, his features had softened, his lips parted, revealing his perfect, white teeth. 'I'll see you tomorrow.' But the sparkle that she longed to see in his eyes was gone.

Chapter Eleven

Sapphire woke to the sound of a dog whining. In her fuzzy, dream-like state, she jumped out of bed to respond to Winston, but as her bare feet hit the frosty floor of the cabin, she remembered with a sudden jolt that she wasn't at home. And Winston wasn't here. As her hands ached to rub his tummy and scratch under his neck, she heard the whimper again.

Moving through the cabin, she flung open the front door. The welcome mat was bare, and a glance at the left and right revealed nothing. But she heard the cry again. She must be going mad. It sounded like Winston wailing for attention, a mix between a growl and youngish mewling. Ignoring the yearning tugging at her heart at the thought of her beloved dog, Sapphire walked to the rear of the house and opened a small, narrow door that led to a courtyard. The bright, early morning sun blinded her.

Squinting, she stepped outside to a loud yelp. Sapphire jumped and hit the timber-panelled wall at the side of the house.

A white ball of fluff was curled into the corner of the doorframe, licking the paw she'd stood on. It was a tiny wee thing that continued to cry.

'Oh.' Her cheeks flushed despite the coolness outside, and she bent to her knees and held out her hand for the animal to sniff. It reared back at first, but then its small, black button nose twitched and ran along one of her fingers, enjoying the new scent. Sapphire slowly moved her hand to its back and petted its spine, the fur soft and thick with a distinct curl. It had to be a poodle mix. Its face looked up at her, and her chest swelled. This dog was almost identical to Winston! How was that even possible? Across the globe and thousands of miles away from home, and outside her door was a stray dog that resembled her Shmoodle.

But where was its mother? Sapphire rose and searched around, racing to the edge of the courtyard and peering over the low fence to the side. The puppy followed at her heels. But together, they didn't discover a lost mummy dog.

The dog licked at her heels. Could it be any cuter? With no hesitation, she scooped it up and held it to her chest, inhaled the sweet animal scent and let the softness of its coat lean against her cheek. The homesickness hit hard and fast, and her chest ached. For home, for comfort, for security and her Winston, who loved her unconditionally and had been her most loyal companion in the last few years. Winston's love had sustained her through the dark days.

The puppy didn't fight her advances, so she snuggled it tighter and moved inside. 'Let's get you something to eat and drink,' she said as she nuzzled its neck.

Inside, she found a small bowl and poured some milk.

Without much food in the pantry, she cooked scrambled eggs and halved them with the dog. The dog lapped it up quicker than her.

After eating, the pup came and leaned against her leg. 'What am I going to do with you, hey? I can't leave you here alone. What about your mumma? She'll be missing you.' With the inclement weather of Hallstatt, she couldn't leave the poor thing outside—anything but. Quickly dressing, she scooped it up, carried it like a toy out the door and headed to the factory.

'What's that dog doing in here?'

Geez, that was quick. Jamie's voice was brash. She'd hidden the precious pup in the corner in a comfy woollen bed she'd purchased on her way. It had settled down for a nap, and Sapphire thought she'd have a few hours before being sprung.

'Jamie, it's . . . it's mine.'

'What?'

'I found the dog this morning and couldn't leave it and didn't know what else to do with it . . . I had to bring her with me.'

'What?' his tone rose as he threw his gaze between her and the puppy.

She wasn't going to repeat the words and sound like a total twat. So, she didn't reply. His head turned in the direction of the dog, who, as if it knew they were talking about it, raised her head, looked at them and offered up the cutest whimper. Whether it was those gorgeous dark eyes or the grumbles, Jamie approached and petted her head. She didn't like that contact, so he petted her under its neck and tummy. Dutifully, the puppy rolled over and held its legs aloft. Jamie chuckled, and Sapphire let out a sigh.

'She looks like Winston.' He turned his head back towards her.

Sapphire nodded.

'Do you still have him?' he asked, his tone softer and lighter now with a touch of whimsy.

'What! Of course.'

'Is, is he okay?'

'He's great. He's a great little dog.' All the while, Jamie kept patting the dog, who lapped up each stroke.

'She was on my doorstep this morning. She must have a mother. Do you have an animal welfare group like the RSPCA over here?'

'I have no idea.' With one hand still stroking the dog, he used the other to make a call. He spoke briefly, and within seconds, a lady entered the kitchen.

'Audrey,' he addressed his secretary in English, 'can you make some enquiries about a lost puppy, not many weeks old by the look of it and found.' He rattled off the address of the cabin. 'Let us know if you find anything out.'

Audrey left, and minutes passed, and Jamie kept his attention on the puppy, who'd now rolled over and was tugging at his shirt sleeve and play-biting.

Memories rushed at Sapphire, and she caught her breath. Winston was their dog. They'd chosen and purchased him together; both loved him. He was the third in their trio. And like everyone else, Jamie had left him, too.

But just as soon, the flick switched, and Jamie rose and, with one last glance, moved away.

Sapphire spent the day in the kitchen making artisan chocolates by herself. One eye was trained on the door, waiting, hoping for Jamie to return, for them to bake together, to create something special. Her other eye was on the puppy she'd christened Winnie after Jakob had visited once word had spread around the factory about their special visitor. Other members of staff drifted in over the day, taking turns to feed her and take her outside to do her business. She had a placid and playful nature, and everyone adored her immediately. There were jokes that she could become the company mascot, an idea Sapphire whole-heartedly agreed with, only if they couldn't find her mother.

Late in the day, Sapphire sought out Audrey and asked about her progress in finding its owner. She shook her head. 'Nothing. I've contacted everyone, and there is no report of a missing puppy or a mother having recently given birth. I'm sorry.'

'That's okay. Thank you for trying.'

Sapphire had decided that she'd done enough for today and was planning to collect Winnie and depart for home. The door to the kitchen was open, and she peered in, worried Winnie might have wandered off.

Jamie lay on the floor with the dog on his chest, its long, slim, and pink tongue lapping at him. He roughed the puppy up with tummy tickles, lifted her into the air and rolled over and around with her as she play-chased him.

Sapphire's chest lurched, and she clutched her hands together. Was the real Jamie still hiding in there? It was a bit of a roller coaster trying to predict which man you'd get at any given moment, but watching him roll around with the dog convinced her. A thought had been simmering at the back of her mind, but seeing him with the dog, she knew. He'd forced himself to become someone else after he moved away. The question was—why would he do that?

Chapter Twelve

A text arrived that night.

I'm taking you to Grindelwald head office tomorrow in Lucerne, Switzerland. We're leaving early, and we'll be gone overnight; be ready.

James

Chapter Thirteen

'Miss Sapphire.' James's driver spoke as he leaned into the rear of the Bentley, where Sapphie was curled into the corner. She was fast asleep, her head resting against the windowpane. One hand lay on the seatbelt sash, and her pink rosebud lips were slightly parted. Winnie snored in her lap.

She'd brought the dog? A flair of irritation spiked but quickly fizzled away. Of course, she'd bought the dog; James should have known. So like her.

His guilt ebbed away at seeing her sleeping. He should have collected her himself. Instead, he'd sent his driver to transport her to the airport, over an hour from Hallstatt. It was a cowardly move, he agreed, but an hour trapped in a confined space with her would have either been torture or ecstasy, and he never knew which. Plus, there'd be plenty of time together throughout the next couple of days.

She must be exhausted. It was such a long trip across the

world, and since her arrival, the days had been gruelling. Today was an extra early start.

With a gentle caress to her shoulder, she roused, and her eyes opened wide in confusion before she stretched out her limbs. As awareness dawned as to where she was, James moved back into position, lined up with the rest of the team at the head of the red carpet he'd rolled out specially.

Sapphie rubbed her eyes before she exited the car, holding the puppy to her chest. Her gaze was glassy until she saw them: Marcus and Lina and the rest of the PR team stood waving and cheering. In true Sapphie style, her eyes opened even wider, if that was possible, before she looked over her shoulder, checking who on earth the fuss was for.

Lina handed her a bouquet and kissed her on both cheeks. They chatted, but James couldn't hear the words. Sapphire's head shook from side to side, and her lips mouthed 'no' before she scanned the assembled group.

'First time on the circuit, and you sell out the chocolates, huh? What's your secret? Is there something special you're not telling us?' Marcus joked and fell back into line after giving her a brotherly pat on the arm. Lina petted Winnie. Graciously, Sapphire accepted the congratulations and cheers, and soon enough, slowly, she stood in front of him at the head of the line.

She truly was a sight for sore eyes, as the old cliché went.

'Congratulations, Sapphire. Your chocolates sold out overnight. That hasn't happened since my arrival. Not in the more expensive artisan range, anyway. Word of mouth spreads quickly in this town. But it wasn't only local orders, either. We've had web orders from across the border.'

He let the words sink in. Sapphie appeared stunned, her face frozen into a smile while she stood stock-still. She looked away from him first and dipped her head into the fluffy fur of the dog before smelling the blossoming buds of edelweiss she held. The world could have opened up and swallowed him right then, and he wouldn't have taken his eyes off her as she inhaled the scent of the blooms.

'Is this the response each time you make a good sale?' She cracked her first smile of the morning. The girl he knew was back.

He retaliated in kind. 'We do like to make a big deal of things, especially wonderful achievements worth celebrating.' Leaning down close, he said, 'Can you believe it? Everyone loved the slabs so much we might have to adopt your recipe.'

Quick as a whip, she replied, 'I'm holding those recipes as confidential information, my secret weapon.' James couldn't tell if she was joking, probably not, so he offered her a smirk instead. One point to Sapphire Banks. 'Your plane awaits.' He gestured to their left.

'Jamie, I had no choice but to bring Winne, she's too little to be left alone. Are you okay with that?'

He paused mid-step and gazed at the dog. 'Winnie?'

'The female version of Winston.'

'It's perfect,' and he continued walking, shouted over his shoulder, 'It's fine she can tag along.'

Marcus and Lina congratulated her again, and patted her on the arms and back, said how wonderful she was etcetera. Lina took the obligatory photographs, this time including Winnie, and filmed a small clip. Sapphire sailed through it. She was either getting used to the attention or wasn't fully awake enough to make a fuss. The remainder of the team said farewell.

'They're not coming with us?' she questioned.

He shook his head to answer no and lead her forward. They traversed the red carpet. Sapphie paused, cast a glance back, then offered a last wave. They ascended the staircase to the small jet plane, and he helped her with her belongings before giving the flowers to a member of the flight crew. She headed to the rear of the plane.

'No, this way,' he said, grasping her elbow and they went to the cockpit where he sat and started fiddling with knobs and panels.

Sapphire stood in the doorway. 'Come in,' he said, 'sit down and buckle up.'

'You aren't the pilot,' she said, swivelling on the spot and checking her surroundings waiting for the real pilot to appear.

He laughed. 'Sure am. There's a few new tricks I've learned since we last saw each other.'

'This isn't a trick, this is . . . this is . . . huge.'

The cabin crew attended to alleviate Sapphire of the luggage that she continued to clutch tightly and offered her a drink of orange juice. The male and female stewards did a double take at the dog before gushing over her, as well. She'd never flown with a dog. Well, in fact, she'd never been flown by a pilot she knew and never seated in the cockpit.

'Okay, I can accept you're the pilot. Lots of people learn how to fly planes, but please tell me, this isn't your plane, is it?'

'Yes, it is.'

She landed with a thump in the passenger seat and sipped her drink.

Now seated, he talked through the headphones and flicked more switches. As if realising this was for real and they were taking off, Sapphire frantically searched for her belt wrapped it around herself, and clutched Winnie.

'Okay, are your comfortable? You can sit back in the suites but I thought because there's only the two of us, you might like to sit up with me. You ready?'

She nodded.

'It's a five-hour flight or thereabouts, depending on the headwinds. We have a selection of pastries and tea and coffee that will be served once we're in the air. I can relax a bit more then.'

Fifteen minutes later, they were cruising amongst the clouds. 'Flying this time of day is pretty special.' James indicated the rising sun, lighting up the world. He kept his eyes ahead but continued, 'Sapphire, I know you think that fanfare back there was over the top, but the feedback we've had on the chocolate is astonishing. People are saying it's the best they've had. I'm trying not to take that personally. But I meant what I said: you are simply incredible. Talented.'

'Stop it. Don't do that. You don't need to flatter me or offer praise or rewards. Is this what this is?'

'No.' His words were forceful. 'This is how I travel to head office. That's where I'm taking you. But forget about that, you're entitled to luxury, aren't you?'

Her face squeezed too tight; her features compacted. Sapphie never liked to be out of her comfort zone. The air steward arrived with a tray of delectable treats, and Sapphie grinned as she made her choices and offered some to Winnie. He urged her to have one of each and ordered an espresso. Excepting they were in a private jet flying across the continent of Europe, it was like old times.

Sometimes, like now, being with Sapphire was like putting on your favourite, well-worn pair of jeans: an incredibly comfortable fit, easy to wear and familiar. His heart ached at the memory of them, her. But back then, before, they were innocent and naïve to think their enchanted life could continue. Nothing was that easy. They were older now, wiser. Tainted by real life. The hard edge he detected early on in Sapphie was more prominent now, even the way she sometimes spoke to him with scorn and scepticism. Not that he didn't deserve it. But the girl he knew loved life, was positive, optimistic and above all, kind, and that had changed.

For the moment, he'd enjoy wearing those old jeans and pretend all was well.

Jamie held the glass door open and gestured for her to enter. The cold blast of air hit her first, but then she saw the chocolate. She turned around, aware her face displayed childish delight and her smile wide and captivating, to capture his reaction. Her enthusiasm must have been infectious, and he rewarded her with his own dazzling grin, no doubt waiting for this reaction.

In the centre of the foyer to the head office of Grindelwald in Lucerne, Switzerland—her second country—was a giant melting pot of chocolate. A waterfall of dark liquid cascaded from the ceiling, curving down and around a five-pointed star and pooling into a fountain-like base. Skipping ahead along with many others entering the building, she peered down and around the base seeking out its exit point. She had to hold Winnie back from jumping straight in. No blaming the little dog, she'd like to lose herself in a large bowl of chocolate, too.

'This is incredible.' She gave Jamie a sideway look of utter disbelief.

'Sure is. And it never gets old. Sometimes I stand here and simply watch people's reactions as they enter. Kids want to stick their fingers in the flow immediately and adults stare in wonder. Even if I wanted to, we can't replicate this at home with the same effect. I mean,' he spread his arms wide, 'look at this place. It's next level in wow factor.'

Sapphire looked around the entry. It was big, wide, high and spacious, with multi-levels and staircases and balconies, complete in a white wonderland, on the walls, the tiles on the floor gleamed shiny and polished and the trims like the banister on the spiralling staircases was silver making the rich dark chocolate stand out even more. Tourists milled around, queues formed to buy tickets and all the while, the unmistakable sickly aroma of sweet sugar hung in the air. What an entrance to the museum and factory.

'This is pretty much the heart of chocolate in Europe, right?' she asked.

'Well, I think so, and Grindelwald will agree. This company is synonymous with exquisite chocolate and are one of the biggest sellers here on the continent and around the world. They amassed the greatest sales last year and did for the previous five years before that.' He moved to stand closer to her, and she got a waft of his fragrance; it overpowered even the chocolate and momentarily disarmed her, and the grin she'd been wearing dropped. He smelled so good that she immediately wanted to melt into him and lose herself there, somewhat like the chocolate surrounding them. James continued, unaware of the effect he had on her. 'There are many chocolatiers across the continent and in the United Kingdom and some of them make remarkable products, but these guys, honestly, are the best.'

'Hence why you're part of their team.'

'Absolutely. But not only their chocolate produce; they are smart entrepreneurs and business people in the modern world, not in the dark ages like some.'

'Like Hinterland, you mean?'

'That's different; they're not in Europe to start with.'

Sapphire wasn't convinced by his sentiment. The factory at home must appear draconian to him if this was the world he inhabited.

A man arrived and slapped him on the back. Another, a stylish woman with hair pulled back severely into a tight bun, wearing an all-white tailored pencil skirt and jacket, kissed him on the cheek. Other staff members waved. Everyone knew him. And liked him.

And why not? Today, his stubble was two days past a shave, but it contrasted perfectly with his dark navy suit. Anyone else might not wear office attire when piloting a plane and visiting head office, but not James. He fitted in perfectly with his seam-creased trousers and suit jacket with a pale lemon shirt and an ice blue tie. With his dark hair and eyes, he presented as dreamy and exotic as if he was about to prance down a catwalk. No wonder the eyes of every woman in the close vicinity were staring in his direction. Including her.

She considered her choice of clothes today—a simple yellow summer dress with spaghetti straps, white cardigan and wedges. There was nothing wrong with it, but arriving here, suddenly, it didn't seem good enough, sophisticated enough, or as glamorous as those around her. Everyone in Europe was always so presentable and polished, like none of them had a grey pair of track pants hidden in their wardrobe to wear while slouching in front of the television! Puffing out her chest a little, she tried to own it. She didn't know anyone so what difference did it make? But she took two steps to her left to create distance between her and Jamie. His sophisticated appearance next to her only acerbated her dowdiness.

'I've arranged a private tour for you,' he announced as another woman in the same white uniform arrived and offered Sapphire a red-lipped smile.

'You're not coming?' She gripped his arm at the elbow.

Jamie raised his eyebrows, and she swiftly released him. Urgh, she hated being so needy! But she was going to be left alone in this alien place with its pristine appearance and robotic-like staff who dressed alike and were *so beautiful...*

'No, I have some business to attend to, but I'll be here when you've finished.'

Sapphie held up Winnie. 'I promise I'll take great care of her,' he said, and while she believed him, she held Winnie extra tight for her last cuddle. Jamie wandered away with a small group, and being alone, her chest tightened and stomach churned. Think of the chocolate, she told herself and followed blindly behind her escort.

Chapter Fourteen

'Hold those thoughts,' Jamie held his hand up to Sapphie, whose mouth was open ready to debrief after her tour. 'Here's a sandwich from the café. Let's get going; I'm taking you somewhere special.'

Sapphie had raced out of the headquarters but paused at his words, pulling up short. She still bounced on her toes with a grin frozen in place. He sensed her excitement, the thrill at what she'd seen, and that delighted him. The thrill of making her happy made him delirious, and that was a drug he wanted to thrive on.

Despite her obvious glee, her mouth closed, and her hand crept to her right arm. She fingered the bangle he now knew dangled there. No hiding it today in her sleeveless dress. Would she trust him? She had once. During their relationship, she'd predominately been the organiser of things to do, places to go, and food. Not that they'd done a lot, to be fair, but with working and family commitments and living in a small town, they'd usually travel to the beach on the weekend or head out for brunch. But Sapphie had always preferred to be in control and not caught by surprise.

Home.

Memories he'd suppressed for years kept surfacing and catching him unawares. His breath caught in his throat.

'Where are we going?' Already, she had reached for the ball of fluff and nuzzled Winnie's face into her neck.

'You'll have to wait and see. Your plane awaits, m'lady,' and he ushered her forward. She stopped.

'We're flying again?'

'Yes, is that okay?'

She shrugged. 'Is that the way you get around now, by plane?'

He paused. 'Well, not in the village, of course; the plane doesn't fit, and there's nowhere to land it. I hardly even use my car there. But the continent is a small place, and it is easy to get around if you have your own transport.'

'Would you fly it to Australia?'

'I could, but it's a long way.'

Sapphire nodded.

'I'd probably get someone to fly it for me.'

She hit him square on the arm, and he chuckled, making a boyish and unfamiliar sound.

'*Oh la,*' she teased as she raced up the plane steps, clutching Winnie tight.

'See, I told you.' Sapphire grinned. 'What's the point of flying when the closest airport is an hour away and then we have to get the train to another car-free village?'

'It would have taken a lot longer if we didn't fly, smarty-pants.'

'What is it with these car-free villages? Is this a European thing?' Sapphire asked as they alighted the train.

'Look around you. Isn't what you see the answer?'

The beauty of Europe still astonished her. Before them was a picturesque town, another toy-doll hamlet with paved paths, narrow alleyways, quaint shops, and upbeat happy music playing. 'We're still in Switzerland, right? We haven't crossed any borders?'

Jamie shook his head, answering no. 'This is a ski town. It's covered in snow during winter, and the skiing is world-class.'

'You've tried it, of course?'

'Of course, and you are today, too.'

She laughed. He had to be joking. It was the end of the European summer; you can't ski in September. He was funny. Jamie pointed to the top of the mountain, and sure enough, there were white peaks.

'Zermatt is open for skiing every day of the year. How unique is that? Says something, right? Incredible, still blows me away.' He hurried her on, and they entered a store where he handed over their belongings and gestured to the staff.

'Pick out whatever gear you'd like, and then we'll fit you for some skis.'

'Should I gather your belongings together, Mr White?' a member of staff asked him as they fussed around, shoving jackets and scarves into her arms.

'Yes, thank you. See you in five,' he said to her.

Three hours later, with the sun still blazing high in the sky, Sapphire followed Jamie, and they skied down a small trail and came to a stop outside a traditional Swiss chalet with smoke billowing out of its chimney. Those traditional flower boxes adorned the window trims, and a bright white and red Swiss flag hung with pride over the door.

They stuck their skis and poles into a mound of snow and headed indoors. Upon entry, they were handed a hot chocolate. Sapphire accepted it with thanks but remained sceptical about chocolate products she hadn't made. One sip and her eyebrows rose in surprise. Jamie caught the gesture and laughed. 'I know, so good.'

They were seated at a corner table with an expansive view out over the mountain with the sun casting a golden glow over the white-covered slopes. The waiter placed napkins over their laps and handed Jamie the drinks menu. He didn't read it and ordered a bottle from memory.

'I hope Winnie is okay,' she muttered, her frown burrowing.

'She is going to be fine. I've arranged for her to have the best care while we are out and . . .' He stretched out his words, 'for her to be doggy-pampered with instructions to buy a new kit of all the essentials she needs.'

Sapphire's grin was wide. 'And what does she need exactly?'

'Well, I'm no expert, but perhaps a jacket for when it's cool, blankets for sleeping, a brush and comb, gourmet treats. I suspect the list is endless. Especially when there's an unlimited budget.'

'Thank you. I don't mind you spoiling her at all.'

'See that mountain over there?' he asked, pointing out the window.

Sapphire craned her neck to see where he aimed. 'Yep.'

'That's the famous Matterhorn.'

She smiled, broad and wide. 'It's so majestic and austere, standing there alone.' The narrow peak was tall and treacherous-looking, covered in milky-white snow and cresting like a wave. 'I've done and seen so much in this past week; I can't believe it.'

'What did you think of Grindelwald HQ?'

'Oh my gosh, I loved it. I l-o-v-e being surrounded by people who adore chocolate as much as I do.' She curled her fingers in and out atop the table with its white linen and crystal glasses. 'But really, I want to make it. Handcraft a special piece, delicately temper the chocolate to the exact temperature, let it cool, check its smooth edges and inhale its scent before adding the final touches, whether that be pistachio, raspberry or a hand-made motif.' Glancing out the window, she continued, 'There's a risk with a company the size of Grindelwald, where everything is made on the production line, and when you're making mass-produced products, you lose the authentic, homemade quality.' She could hear the protestations about to erupt from Jamie and held up her hand. 'I'm not denying their chocolate is fabulous, but I prefer smaller scale, unique and individual. There is nothing better than opening a box of finely crafted bite-sized artisan chocolate.'

Jamie nodded. 'You agree?'

'Sure. There's nothing like it. I guess I'm trying to find a happy medium. The exclusive range is still handmade, as you've experienced yourself. That is art.'

'Yeah, it is in terms of flavour. But making slab chocolate isn't the same. It's easier, less articulate, right?'

'Yeah, but it's a compromise between bigger quantities and not machine-made.'

'Sure . . .' The sommelier arrived and showed the bottle of wine to Jamie. There was a show of holding the glass up to the light, swirling the liquid, and taste testing until Jamie agreed it was acceptable. It was poured, and they each took a sip before speaking again.

Sapphire enjoyed the warm, rich, red mixture and checked the wine on the drinks menu. 'This wine is two hundred and fifty Swiss Francs. Jamie, that's ridiculous. What's that on Australian conversion?' Scrabbling for her phone, she pulled it out and opened the calculator. 'That's almost four hundred Australian dollars. Jamie, no, send it back,' she said and pushed her full glass across the table.

'Don't be ridiculous. This is a vintage wine from a vineyard in Tuscany that I love. Marcello Wines. Savour it, enjoy the flavour, its richness and the deep plum tones.'

It was impossible not to stare dumbfounded. 'You sound like an upper-class tosser.' But she took a large gulp as if to prove a point.

Bread fresh out of the oven arrived, and her tummy rumbled. She'd had nothing since the quick sandwich after her tour. She immediately slathered a slice of bread with butter. 'To line my stomach,' she explained.

They ordered and waited for the waiter to leave before talking again.

'There's only one thing,' she said through a mouthful of bread. Jamie frowned. 'You want more bread? I can request some.' He held up his hand for the waiter's attention.

'No!' She tugged his hand down onto the table and gazed at it for a moment too long as a tingle raced up her arm. Her eyes locked on his, and luckily, he was distracted by the very attentive wait staff. 'Oh, sparkling water, please.'

Ignoring the flush of heat creeping up her neck, she continued. 'I asked my guide at the factory about where they sourced their beans. She gave an impressive and informed spiel about location and quality but she denied the use of child labour. Jamie, the plantations your company uses are on the Ivory Coast. It's infamous for using children as slaves. It's rife and well-known in the industry.'

'No.' He shook his head, and a few curls bounced. 'It was, but Africa and the largest chocolate manufacturers around the world have signed a treaty to declare they won't tolerate child labour anymore.'

'Has Grindelwald?'

Jamie sipped his drink. 'I'm sure they are in agreement with it...'

'But you don't know for sure.'

Another sip, longer and deeper. 'No, now that you mention it, I'm not one hundred percent sure.'

She sighed. 'You haven't asked about Hinterland. Are you interested?'

A patchwork of emotions crossed his face and Sapphire couldn't work out what it meant. Confusion, worry, anxiety, regret, guilt. It was all there. What did that mean? 'They started your career, remember. You wouldn't be here today without them, without the training Seb gave you.'

He placed his arm along the top of the table so that their hands almost connected. The slightest of movements and their pinkies would be linked. Jamie hung his head. 'I know that. I will be forever grateful for that opportunity.'

'I know they seem lame to you now, but it's been tough.' Her voice cracked.

His frown deepened. 'Why? What do you mean?'

'Seb took the ethical sourcing of his beans seriously. Like we all should. Anyway, he investigated the issue and morally couldn't promote chocolate that was made and marketed off the backs of children who should have been in school and instead were working long, difficult days on farms. And illegally. Despite what the African government says, the conditions on cocoa farms remain poor, and many of them still use children. I watched this documentary; I'll show you.'

It took a few minutes, but she found the video and played it on her phone in the centre of the table. It was too long in its entirety, but she sped up to the part where a boy of about ten had been duped into going with smugglers onto a bus, and there was a scene when he'd realised that he'd been stolen to work the fields for chocolate makers. He was alone and crying with no one to help him. It was heartbreaking the first time, but once again, she couldn't believe such terrible things had happened in their modern world. There were many distressing parts to the film: the children working long days in the heat to farm the cacao, the prices sought and bribes taken, and the heavy tactics of the local government. It appeared to be an abhorrent and unregulated industry despite what was being projected to the rest of the world. She'd done her own research too, of course.

Turning it off, she said, 'We can replay the whole thing later. Anyway, Seb decided he couldn't be part of an industry that operated like that. So, he located organisations that guarantee the source of the cocoa. These are fair trade organisations, and they ensure the beans come from farms where the workers are paid a fair price for the produce, and have rights and protections. Like any Western country. Fairtrade pays a minimum price, and of course, they do not use children for labour.'

'Anyway, long story, but Seb decided to adopt these practices. The entire company was in support, excited, and happy with the approach. It was right, and we all felt good about it, as if we were responsible global citizens. That decision was made, and we transferred our product and supply chain at the start of 2020. I'm sure you understand that in any climate, it is a risk because when you pay more for your ethically sourced chocolate from the right places, the price of our products has to, in return, increase. It's not possible to pay a fair and proper price for the cocoa and on-sell for the prices we were. That meant we lost some business. Seb was aware this was a likelihood, understood it, and was prepared. It was a long-term goal. But three months later, COVID hit, and everyone was doing it tough. Luxuries were the first things people cut back on, and more expensive, ethical chocolate wasn't high on anyone's priority list. Sales dropped drastically. The pandemic lasted longer than anyone expected and it's been tough ever since. He hasn't—the company—hasn't quite recovered.'

'I didn't know. Is that why you're here? He's trying to find you another job?'

She held her hand up with a flat palm and cut him off. 'No! How could you think that? Other than him, I'm the only choco-latier at the factory. I can't leave, unlike you who up and left... and then never kept in touch.' Her words were harsher than she intended. His foot accidentally brushed hers under the table, and another jolt vibrated straight up her leg and reached her core. She shifted her foot under her chair.

Their meals arrived, diffusing the building tension. The restaurant filled up, and snatches of conversation were heard, along with the clinking of glasses and crockery. Jamie remained silent for a long while.

'I know!' He almost jumped out of his chair. 'Let's find out. Let's fly to Africa and see these plantations for ourselves. Do our own investigating. It's not that far...'

Covering her mouth full of the most delicious schnitzel she'd ever tasted, she laughed, trying not to spill the food out of her mouth. 'Don't be ridiculous!'

'No seriously. Let's do it. We can be there tomorrow.'

She shook her head more violently. 'It's hard to take you seri-ously. Yes, you might have the ability to be there tomorrow, but if you're interested, you need to do your groundwork first. Do you even know where the plantations are that supply Grindels?'

'Grindels?'

'Grindelwald is such a mouthful,' she said deadpan.

'I'd forgotten the Aussies shorten and place everything into slang.'

You wouldn't have forgotten if you'd kept in touch. She wanted to scream but ate her potato salad instead.

'I'm sorry the company's been doing it tough.' He looked at her over his lashes and batted them in the now-darkening room.

Whilst they'd been talking, someone had lit candles along the windowsills, and the restaurant had a warm, tender glow. Jamie's face, etched with concern, blazed in the amber light.

They ate in silence. A well of concern opened up in Sapphire, and she ached for her job and the future of the company, and here with Jamie, she couldn't help but wonder, if he'd stayed, would things have turned out differently? As the chief chocolatier, he'd have had a say in the produce used. She shook her head, shaking away those thoughts. Useless. There'd been so many "what ifs" over the years; it was exhausting.

It was dark when they finished their meals. As they exited into the cold night air, Sapphire panicked. 'Jamie, how are we going to get down? It's dark, and we can't ski.'

'It's okay,' he said, placing an arm around her waist. Her insides turned to mush, and she willed her body to obey her command and not respond to the tantalising feel of him so close. It ignored her, and her skin buzzed with his touch. 'I've arranged for someone to collect our skis and deliver them to the lodge. And we're getting a lift.' He pointed. Her eyes adjusted, and she spotted a skidoo.

'Please don't tell me you own that, too?' she pleaded.

'Not this time, I've hired it.'

He moved away towards the ski vehicle, and his arm dropped from her waist. Her body sagged. From relief or disappointment? Probably both, but it was safer if he kept his hands to himself.

He waited at the skidoo, holding open the clear door. She stepped inside, and he followed. Knees knocked, and legs touched as they squished into place, Jamie in the driver's seat and her directly behind.

The door shut, and they were alone. She heard her breath, and her chest rose and fell. She was conscious of each part of her body that connected with his. With her hands aloft, not sure where to put them, she searched the sides of the tiny vehicle for handholds, a door handle, anything for her to grasp. Nothing. She placed them on her thighs, but that didn't work.

Jamie inhaled and a strange little whistle emitted from his nose on the out-breath. It was all she heard until the vehicle roared to life. Jamie revved heavily, and they shot forward, scooting down the hill. The velocity jolted her backwards, and she reached for his middle before clutching tight to avoid being sloshed around the small interior. He stiffened momentarily, and then his body relaxed, and she leaned in.

It was like a roller coaster ride as they headed straight down the incline. At each turn, their bodies followed the route, and her breasts squished against his back. Launching over a bump, she squealed, held tighter and buried her head into his back, covering her eyes. His hand lifted from the handlebars and moved toward hers, but at the last minute, he retracted it.

Try to hate him. But that was ridiculous. An impossible task, damn it. And now they were pushed together once again, and she couldn't get away. Did she even want to? She loved being this close to him and wished desperately that she didn't. The feel of him, his movements, his touch, the warmth radiating off his back, and his scent. Yep, she was pretty much in her happy place right now. Damnit, she was only human. And yes, she hated the person he'd become, but in instances like these, he resembled the boy she'd once loved. And how she'd loved him fiercely. Sapphire closed her eyes and rested her chin on his left shoulder. Nothing could take away from this moment.

Arriving at the edge of town, the vehicle skidded to a stop. Jamie held the door open once again and seized the tips of her fingers as she alighted. Asphyxiating from the lack of oxygen, she stumbled, and his arms encircled her body to prevent her fall.

Bloody hell.

Everything occurred in slow motion. Jamie continued to hold her after she'd stabilised and found her feet. Their bodies contacted groins dangerously close, and she willed herself not to look up. Because if she did, she'd be a goner. But of course, her body disobeyed, and she slowly glanced at him, trying to appear nonchalant, his face only centimetres from hers. His warm breath brushed her cheeks, his lips parted, hers did in response, but she needed some air; she couldn't breathe; her jacket was too tight around her neck, and then . . .Jamie dropped his arms and shifted, leaving a gulf of distance between them.

Longing had been building between them, not helped by the activities they'd engaged in that required them to touch: tandem skiing, riding in skidoos, and cable cars, chairlifts and in cockpits all requiring close proximity. And then there were the shared meals, candlelit restaurants with expensive red wine and open log fires along with the endless exchange of seductive shy smiles, and glances under lashes, topped off with a romantic location. And in one movement, one second of time, it was gone, like the popping of a bubble. She did hate him. If it wasn't for him and what he'd done, she wouldn't be here, in this position, berating herself for liking him, switching between loathing him and loving him, not wanting to be near him, and only wanting to be in his presence.

Only to be rejected. It hurt, and she wished it didn't. Did he not want to kiss her? Have her body against his and quell the burning desire within?

Obviously not.

Without a word, he commenced walking and they covered the short distance to the lodge side by side with plenty of space between them.

When they entered their accommodation, the staff swiftly opened the doors and offered a range of five-star services and . . . what, one room?

She turned to Jamie, panic settling in and causing her heart to race. 'I'm really sorry,' he said, 'they only had one room left. We'll have to share.' The foyer was too warm and closed in around her. But instead of giving in to the sensation, she nodded her head in silent agreement.

'Sapphire, I'm sorry,' he said again in the tiny lift, taking them to the tenth floor.

Was everything small in this country?

'But don't worry. European hotel rooms always have single beds that they push together. We'll be fine.' He offered a tight smile but it didn't reassure her at all. He was worried about the bed when all she wanted was for him to kiss her, hold her tight, and never let go . . .

Swiping the key card across the lock, the door opened. Soft, classical music filled the dimly lit room. Candles burned along the window ledge. Jamie found the lights, and the room illuminated. Red, white, and pink rose petals were scattered across the perfectly white and crisp bed and around the beige carpet. In the corner sat a timber spa bath with a bottle of champagne poking out of ice in a bucket.

'Shit,' Jamie muttered. 'They've given us the honeymoon suite.' He lifted the duvet cover and tugged at the timber frame of the bed. 'And there's only one bed.'

Chapter Fifteen

Sapphie was so close it was unbearable. James concentrated on his own heartbeat banging in his ears to ensure he stayed still and avoided touching one single strip of her smooth bare skin. His body was stiff, amongst other things, and he lay on his side, turned away.

It wasn't even as if she'd changed into her nightclothes and emerged from the salon bathroom wearing a sexy negligee. Sapphire wore flannelette PJs of a long top and shorts. Only her legs were bare. It was normal, standard night apparel, sort of cute if you were having a sleepover at a friend's house. But that was the thing: Sapphie didn't have to wear sexy clothes to be appealing. She simply was. That cute pixie face with matching grin and usually sparkling eyes that gave the recipient their undivided attention. Her kind nature. She projected a childlike innocence but surprised him every day with her inner strength and fortitude. She made him vulnerable with one wistful glance.

And now, in the dark hotel room, she consumed his

thoughts. Her body within reach, her beautiful wide hips that he would grasp during lovemaking, her ample breasts, the nipples pert and prominent through her shirt before she'd covered up and crawled into bed, her toes that he knew would be icy cold, and oh boy, her fresh talcum smell, light and floral...

Stop. Thinking. About. Her.

He'd imagine chocolate instead. No! She was chocolate. The child labour situation in East Africa should sort out his swelling problems, but no! She'd told him about the issue. Okay, Seb, then. No! That's where they'd met and worked. So, James White had not one single coherent thought that did not relate to Sapphire Banks. Great. He'd travelled the world and been away for more than five years and he still couldn't escape. He wouldn't even dream of *home*, whatever that was, because she was intrinsically linked to that, too.

Had he done nothing in the last five years?

Nothing to do then except dream of her laying underneath him, naked, those innocent emerald eyes staring up at him with desire and love. Wanting him. Her caressing the skin on his back, making his body twitch. Him touching her down the curve of her hip, his favourite spot and feeling her twist under him with titillation.

He could do it. He could take her now. And the worst part was, he thought, Sapphie would let him.

Chapter Sixteen

Her skin tingled with goosebumps but she wasn't cold.

Jamie was next to her, sleeping in only boxer shorts. His lean and toned chest was bare. At the sight of him, her mouth had gone dry, and she'd had to clasp her hands tight together to prevent them from reaching out and running her fingers down the hairless skin and over the bump of each ab.

Now, all of a sudden, she wasn't so certain of her plan. Spending time with him to get over him? Ha, right! It seemed ridiculous in the darkness of this room and as each day passed. Her tough facade was fading fast. She was alone and far from home. All she wanted was to be held and cared for. She would not cry! Instead, she hugged the large European pillow close and snuffled into the depth of its filling.

The mattress shifted, and Jamie moved. Her heart beat so fast it hurt in her chest and talons of fear clawed at her belly. What was she afraid of? Not Jamie, but herself.

An arm embraced her middle, the hand tucking back in

under her body. His legs curved along the side of her, fitting perfectly into her grooves. He spooned her, and a wild stab of hope sprouted that just as quickly dampened down. Her mind scattered to a million different places and, simultaneously, none at all. She didn't know how to react.

Did she want him? Yes, but that response was a whisper in her head. Would she let him? No! Her mother and sisters screamed in her ears. No, she wouldn't let him take her, ravage her in this romantic interlude they'd accidentally found themselves in. In a romantic ski chalet on a snow-covered mountain at the base of an idyllic village. The stuff of dreams. She would not be so weak. It would only reward his bad behaviour. She had to hold firm.

Sapphire pretended to sleep, but silently, she willed him to keep cuddling her and stay close. Perhaps she would sleep tonight after all.

Chapter Seventeen

'Darling! You didn't tell me you were going away!'

The long-legged Amazonian goddess rushed towards them on the tarmac but she wasn't heading for Sapphire.

A blur of colour flashed past, the jingle of bangles clashing together and heels, those belonging to knee-high leather boots, clacked on the concrete. A Moulin Rouge red single-breasted coat flapped as she approached revealing a silk cream blouse matched with black slacks. The obligatory oversized handbag was discarded onto the ground before the woman reached her arms up and around Jamie's neck. Her entire look was overshadowed by the most glorious head of luscious, long dark locks Sapphire had most likely ever seen—like out of a shampoo commercial. And yet another example of the beautiful people in this part of the world.

The woman made an exaggerated motion of embracing

Jamie, made noises Sapphire couldn't decipher, and pulled him close as if making sure he wouldn't escape.

Unable to pull her eyes away, she tried to keep her expression neutral, or at least curious, but her eyebrows furrowed and her eyes blinked too many times. Who was she? Instinctively, she clutched Winnie tighter as if that might prevent her from emptying her stomach of the scrumptious breakfast they'd not long ago eaten. What on earth did she do before she found Winnie? Thank goodness for the small dog who had replaced her own Winston for the time being.

How quickly circumstances changed. Last night and this morning were some of the best times she'd shared with Jamie since her arrival. All above board, of course; well perhaps not the spooning but they'd both conveniently not mentioned that and when she'd woken, he was back on his own side of the shared bed.

A smorgasbord of breakfast options had been delivered to the room while she dressed alone with Winnie who was content after her overnight stay in dog luxury. They'd sat indoors before the open bay window and watched skiers heading for lifts and tourists and locals alike enjoying the morning sunshine. It was idyllic. As idyllic as it could be. Sapphire wasn't stupid; she wasn't pretending it was something it wasn't, but it had been pleasant, Jamie had been great company—chivalrous, fun and the most relaxed she'd seen him since her arrival. Okay, nothing about it was real life, but she'd admit it was a nice little interlude where they'd been in a bubble of fun and mutual admiration.

Now, the bubble burst and slammed her hard in the face.

Here was the girlfriend! Sapphire remembered the endless stream of celebrity photographs of James with this model.

Of course, their time together was too good to be true. It now made it seem like pretend. How does one forget to mention a gorgeous-looking girlfriend, out of the pages of a magazine? The pair continued to kiss in front of him. It wasn't obvious whether it was a mutual coming together or she kissed him, but either way, their lips connected and her tummy roiled, and her hand rushed to her mouth.

Jamie pulled back and put both hands on the woman's arms, securing her in place. His body was rigid as they exchanged words, whereas the woman gazed up at him in wonderment and adoration. She brushed the hair back that blew in her face and her shoulders jiggled like she was laughing.

Nausea swirled in Sapphire's stomach as time drew on and the pair didn't separate. She placed Winnie on the ground, safely attached to her new lead and harness. Instead of playing with the dog, Sapphire twiddled her bangle. Sort of inappropriate, given Jamie had given it to her, and here he was kissing another woman in front of her, but you know, habit. Did he gift this woman the numerous accessories she wore? Sapphire fiddled with the hard gold clasp of her bracelet, the action calming her. Then she twirled it one way around her wrist, then the other. The methodical action soothed the swirling feelings within.

They kept talking. Sapphire shuffled her feet. She spied the company Bentley a few metres away. Should she make a run for it? Yes, she decided, and her feet moved. Collecting the handle on her wheelie luggage, she went to make a quick getaway. Her hand reached the car door. 'Sapphie!' and Jamie was behind her, his flat palm to her back.

Damn it! The driver collected her bag and placed it in the boot. With her arms now empty, she swung around to face him.

Jamie was only inches away, too close, cloying. 'Sapphie,' he said, but the woman was behind him. She was tall to Sapphie's short, lean to her shapely figure; glowing and glamorous to her dull complexion and wispy shoulder-length hair; wide beaming, all teeth smile to her tight-lipped grimace.

Jamie was attracted to her? His eyes diverted left and right, his mouth closed, and he swallowed back whatever words he was about to utter. His jaw clenched, and the pulse in his neck beat out of his skin.

The woman rattled off in a language Sapphire didn't recognise, but it wasn't German, and more surprisingly, Jamie replied!

The woman nodded and spoke English. 'I am Valentina,' she said, moving around Jamie and kissing Sapphie on the cheek. 'Usually, in this situation, I would say I've heard so much about you, but that simply isn't the case.' She spoke with a tight smile, and Sapphire wondered what was hiding under the veneer. 'Who are you?' she continued, and her smile became marginally wider and stuck in place. Winnie sniffed at her perfectly painted toenails in high-block sandals, but Valentina ignored her and lifted her foot as if to kick her away. Sapphire yanked on the lead and pulled Winnie to safety.

'Valentina, this is Sapphire Banks. Sapphire, Valentina. She is our Australian mentee, part of the program the company is running at the moment. I'm sure I've mentioned it.'

Valentina didn't play along and shook her head, her hair flying around, the long strands hitting Sapphire on the cheek. But Valentina lost interest quickly, talking rapidly to Jamie and excluding her. One thing she was certain about; she wasn't going to hang around and be part of some lovers' spat. Turning without another word, she got in the car, slammed the door shut and pulled down her sunglasses to hide her distress.

It was mid-morning in the middle of the week at the factory in Hallstatt, and people were scattered about: customers coming and going, workers on breaks and a few tourists if the cameras around their necks were any indication. The Bentley drove away and left her standing at the entrance, luggage beside her, Winnie beside it. For the one-hundredth time in recent memory, she was lost, adrift, so far out of her comfort zone she didn't know where to go or what to do. A muted ringtone played from a distance before her pocket commenced to vibrate.

Pulling out her phone, she recognised the number as home. Her family were Face Timing her. Frantically, she ran her fingers through her hair like a comb, rubbed under her eyes and pinched her cheeks until they hurt. Swiping the screen, she held the phone away from her face, deeply inhaled twice and faced her family with a grin.

Daisy and Olive beamed back, their faces squished into the rectangle frame. They squealed and danced on the spot, and she matched it. Tears caught at the back of her throat, and she swallowed them away. The aching need to reach out and embrace her sisters, her best friends, was great. Luckily, they ambushed her with a hundred questions that provided ample distraction.

'But first, let me introduce,' she said, making a drumroll, 'Winnie, the stray dog I found.'

There were gasps and a few seconds until her Winston

appeared on the screen; the gazes of all three women went back and forth between the two dogs.

'They could be twins!' Olive shouted down the line. Sapphire shoved Winnie toward the phone, ridiculously thinking the dog would get a glimpse of Winston. Perhaps the two would fall in love? That was a stupid thought, and she pulled her back. The dogs were worlds apart.

After the excitement of telling them about the discovery of Winnie, they settled down and spoke normally. 'Actually, I'm at the factory. Want a tour?' she was already entering before they replied with a resounding yes.

With the phone facing outwards, she waltzed through the space showing off different workstations, holding up samples of chocolate, and getting random staff to wave and say *'guten tag'*. She ended up in the kitchen. 'This is where I spend most of my time, learning, in demonstrations, making chocolate.'

'Ooh, fancy,' Daisy said. Most things would appear as impressive to Daisy, who like Sapphire, only until those few short weeks ago, had never left Australia.

But it was time to switch to safer topics: them. 'How are Mum and Dad and Grandma?' she asked.

Her sisters replied, and their images jiggled as they moved, and Winston bounced around. Her eyes watered as she watched her dog, and she attempted some ridiculous baby talk, which he completely ignored. He played with Daisy and Olive instead.

'Put the phone closer,' she demanded and yet he still didn't listen. 'He's forgotten me,' she lamented.

'Don't be daft. He probably can't see you properly. Each

time you talk, he stops, so he's recognising your voice. Keep talking for a bit.'

She tried it, not caring how crazy she sounded. In the midst of her gush and making silly faces at the phone, the door swung open and Lina sauntered in wearing a stunning tan crop top number with tight white pants and high cork wedges that were silent against the polished concrete floor.

Sapphire broke into a grin. 'Lina, come over here and meet my sisters,' she ushered her over with one hand and held up the screen. 'This is my friend, Lina. Lina, these are my sisters, Daisy and Olive.' They waved back and exchanged hellos. 'Lina works in the marketing department here at the chocolate factory and looks after me.'

'You look fabulous; I love your clothes,' Daisy replied, impressed again.

'You've made a friend!' exclaimed Olive, in a tone Sapphire would have preferred she didn't use. Her sisters exchanged incredulous glances and clapped their hands together in glee. Their reaction confirmed what a loser they thought she was, and a jolt of pain crisscrossed her chest at the person they'd love her to be: friendly, outgoing, vivacious, and someone who, well, had friends and, moreover, spent time with other people.

The door swung open again, and a deep voice yelled, 'Delivery for James White, there's no one at the front desk.' Sapphire turned in that direction, reigning in Winnie on her lead; she barked and wanted to bound across to the courier. Lina signed the delivery papers and accepted the package on his behalf. Until...

A screech emanated from the phone at high volume. 'James White!' The name was then repeated at the same level by her other sister. 'Is that *the* James White? Sapphire Banks, it can't be, tell me it isn't. That's impossible. No!'

The sisters talked over each other in a garbled jumble while Lina focused on the parcel. Did she pause at the screech? Did her shoulders pull back? Did she hear?

Sapphire held one solitary finger up to her mouth to shush her sisters, but they weren't getting the message. Lina had the package and walked back across the very small space.

'If that's him, Sapphire, I'm coming over there right now and getting you! Tell us what's going on. What's that ratbag up to? We'll sort him out. Are you alright? This is crazy. Well, I can't believe it...'

No choice but to talk over them. 'Thanks so much for your call; I've got to get going; busy afternoon ahead; love you loads, say hi to Mum and Dad.' She shut down the call, spun the other way and busied herself at the kitchen bench. She needed a moment to collect herself and get a neutral expression on her face. Lina's silent footsteps followed behind her until Sapphire detected her presence.

'They seem nice?' she commented as if a question.

Sapphire spun around too fast, and she stumbled, grabbing the bench for support. 'So n-i-c-e,' she dragged out the syllables.

'They don't like James?'

The question was heavy with innuendo. Sapphire shook her head. 'No, no, not at all, I don't know what they're talking about...'

'But James is from home; you knew him...' More lingering unsaid meaning.

'Oh, yeah, they've met. No big deal. Nothing much happens

back in Canungra, you know small town. People overreact. Everything is exciting.'

'You hadn't told them about seeing James again?'

Sapphire stood and looked directly at her. 'Nothing to tell. James White is not important enough to share.'

Lina considered her but accepted her reply and her weird behaviour. A sharp knife edge pierced Sapphire's heart at the deceit and derogatory words about her hometown and its people.

Lina shuffled some papers in front of her before asking about her trip to head office, as if she'd just remembered.

'It was great.'

'I hope James took some pics for our channel. And that leads me to what you are doing this afternoon.'

Sapphire's hopes soared. She couldn't wait to get back into it, take the wooden spoon in her hand, hold the warm bowl nursing the tepid chocolate, pour and shake and mould and make something beautiful and hopefully delicious.

'We need more,' she said. 'More of you and less of the chocolate. A profile, not only of you but your time here in Hallstatt.'

The excitement dissipated, replaced by a clenching stomach.

'So'—Lina placed one hand on her arm— 'we have a big afternoon planned. We're taking you to the largest attraction in Hallstatt. It's a sacrilege you haven't been there yet and to the lake, too. It's a gorgeous day; the shots will be fabulous.'

'What's the biggest attraction again?'

Lina tutted. 'See! You should know that. It emphasises the importance of our afternoon. The salt mine, of course! Get your stuff and let's get started.'

Chapter Eighteen

'Oh, this is delicious!' Sapphire exclaimed as she sipped the pink cocktail.

'You've never had a piña colada before?' Lina's tone sounded incredulous, but she was probably reading too much into it, and Sapphire shrugged to make light of it.

'It's like a slushie.'

'A what now?' Marcus asked.

'You know, a soft drink that's made with crushed ice and is, well, soft and you slurp it through a straw, hence why it's called a Slurpee. You get them from the 7Eleven.'

Lina and Marcus laughed, leaning back in their seats. 'We don't know what you're talking about, girlfriend, but it can't be as good as these.' Marcus held up his tall glass containing the pink liquid resplendent with strawberries and a cocktail umbrella and shouted "prost" to the group, who drank in unison.

Let them mock. Nothing mattered but where she was, and how she felt. Winnie sat at her feet, fast asleep.

What a day!

Now, she sat drinking with the team on the shores of Lake Hallstatt. It quite possibly might be the most beautiful place on earth, and it was, indeed, the most stunning spot she'd ever been. Granted, she'd been limited places, but she was sure this would remain one of the best. And this was the nicest cocktail she'd ever had, too!

It was late afternoon, but the sun still peeked above the mountain at their backs and behind the town. The bright orange glow of the day had turned into a muted tangerine that lined the horizon. The heat lingered, and unlike most, Sapphire savoured its warm rays on her bare arms and did not find it heavy and oppressive. They sat on a timber pontoon facing the lake that shimmered like a mirror reflecting the beauty of the town. Around her, the mood was jubilant, and she tapped her feet to the beat pulsing from the jukebox and found the cheerful chatter around her lifted her spirits even further.

'I need to duck to the loo. Can you mind Winnie and my stuff, please?' Sapphire placed her jacket and phone on the table. She turned her mobile phone face down and gave Marcus Winnie's leash to hold.

'Of course, no problem,' Marcus waved her away.

Returning, she weaved her way through the thickening crowd and saw Marcus chatting to the group ignoring Winnie as she stood under the table. Lina sat huddled over but straightened as Sapphire climbed onto the bench seat next to her.

'Come here, Winnie.'

The dog raced over, dragging its lead. Her mobile phone sat

face up, and the screen was lit. She was about to pick it up and check when a body pushed against her from the side, and she looked up into Jamie's startling dark eyes. Her tummy swooped, and her heart went all aflutter at his ravishing good looks. The effect he had on her was quite annoying. Then he smiled—dear sweet Lord.

'You made it!' Lina exclaimed.

Her retort was less welcoming. 'How did you know we were here?'

Instead of allowing Jamie to reply, Lina jumped in. 'He's the boss; he knows everything!' and she took another sip of the drink. Her expression was strange, aloof and she avoided Sapphire's eye.

'Boss's shout, I say,' Marcus raised his glass.

'All right,' Jamie agreed and rose. 'Same all 'round?'

'No, I'm good,' she said, holding up her half-drunk piña colada.

'Ah, c'mon.' Lina bumped her shoulder. 'Live a little, get her another one, James.'

Jamie raised an eyebrow in her direction but didn't enquire further. Both Lina and Marcus had already demolished their drinks.

'So, tell me about today,' Jamie asked as he sat back down with the drinks only moments later. The others pounced on theirs and Sapphire quickly sipped to catch up. There was a bowl of nuts in the middle of the table, and she scooped up a handful of them before replying.

'Good,' she exclaimed after chewing. 'The salt mine is incredible. I loved the history of it and how it made this town what it is, and those indoor slides were very cool!'

'Yeah, it's pretty good—'

Lina cut in. 'Except, we only wanted a few photos outside, but Sapphire insisted on taking the full tour that took hours, and we waited and waited...' She rolled her eyes for effect.

'Of course! She's at the most famous tourist attraction in Hallstatt; you're not going to have your photo taken outside and not go in, right?' Jamie said.

Lina didn't reply further.

'You got your photos, didn't you? And probably more than you'll need.' Sapphire said.

'Let's get some more.' Lina nudged the poor photographer's arm as he sat enjoying his own drink after trailing them around all afternoon. He jumped to action, aiming and shooting. Lina directed him to catch shots of her and Jamie, drinks held aloft, their backs to the lake, then the other direction with the houses climbing the incline, the sun in their eyes, with drinks, without drinks, smiling, not smiling.

It was Jamie who finally called it. 'Enough, already, let's enjoy ourselves.'

The camera guy skulled the remainder of his drink and departed with a wave.

'Oh, James, I almost forgot. I think you should see this.' Lina handed over a newspaper. It was written in German, so Sapphire cast her eyes across the glorious lake and watched people water skiing, boating and canoeing.

Next to her Jamie tensed; he lifted the paper higher and held it up to the light. When she glanced across, his brows were knitted, his lips tight as he read.

Doing her best not to appear obvious, she cast her gaze lower to capture the page he read. It was a society page with colour photographs of people doing exactly what they were, drinking and out and about, at some event or other. Then she saw it: the dark hair, long legs, distinct features. Valentina. She was wrapped around another man, their gaze intent on the camera, but their arms linked, legs entwined, her head leaning against his cheek. In another, she sat on his lap, head thrown back in mirth.

Sapphire turned her head to take in Jamie's expression. His jaw was clenched while he glared at the images. Was he hurting? Instinctively, she placed her hand on his thigh, a show of support and solidarity. No one liked to be the victim of a scandal. Lowering his head, he considered her hand, cast a furtive glance in her direction, and folded the paper into perfect squares before placing it on the table. He then reached for his drink, not a strawberry piña colada, some sort of spirit straight up in a stout glass. 'Let's have another drink.'

Sapphire caught Lina's gaze before she squealed like a schoolgirl, and Marcus made a similar masculine response. By instinct, she leaned her body in towards Jamie, so close she felt his body heat. Why exactly had Lina shown Jamie the paper?

'My shout,' Sapphire said and rose. This time she tied Winnie's leash to the leg of the table. Avoiding eye contact with Jamie, she headed towards the bar. It was a tourist spot, she guessed they all were and housed some tacky souvenirs of cups, scarves, hats and T-shirts with Hallstatt emblazoned over them and a stack of postcards on a stand.

She spun the carousel of cards trying to find the most attractive images when her body flooded with warmth and hot breath tickled her ear. 'I didn't tell you what I was drinking.'

Sapphire didn't turn. Her gaze remained on a postcard with a smiling child swooshing down one of the slides in the salt mine, wearing the ridiculous white suit guests were required to don to protect the inner sanctum. The image blurred as all she could focus on was his warm breath, and even though his words weren't tantalising, they rushed heat through her body. He was too close. Distance helped her keep her cool. Now she was trapped between the man she loved to hate and the stand of postcards. She willed her hand forward and extracted a photo of the township covered in snow.

'I'll send this one to your dad.'

For the second time in minutes, his body went stiff. He stepped back, the warmth disappearing, and she sighed in relief.

'My dad?' he queried. 'Why would you be sending a post-card to him?'

'I said I would. It'll make his day.' Sapphire turned the stand.

Jamie reached across and stopped the stand mid-spin. 'You've spoken to him?'

'What do you mean? Of course, I've spoken to him. I've been visiting him since you left.' She paused; should she go on? 'Someone had to,' she spat out but kept her voice low as if he wouldn't hear it.

Gripping her two arms, he turned her to face him. A queue was gathering behind them for the bar. 'No, you do not. I have carers arranged to take care of his every need. There are medical staff, food delivery, cleaners; he does not need for anything.'

'Except company and someone he knows to check on him.'

'How often do you visit?'

She was getting impatient now. 'Every week, Friday after-noon after work.'

'After work?' His voice had taken on a funny croak, and he

cleared it. He stared at the ground as he asked, 'Do you talk about the factory?'

'What? Of course, we do, but we talk about a lot of things.'

'What do you say about the factory? What does he ask?'

Sapphire shook her head. At complaints from behind, he pulled her aside so they were out of the queue of people ordering drinks.

'Stop. Visiting. Him.' He spoke through gritted teeth.

'What? No. Why would you say that? Don't you want to ensure your disabled dad is okay?'

'He is okay because I've made sure of it.'

'By paying strangers to care for him.'

'It's the very best of care.'

'But it's not you.'

He gripped her arm.

'Ow, you're hurting me and, quite frankly, being ridiculous. Jamie.' Sapphire took a deep breath; she never spoke to him like this. It was weird but also exhilarating. 'You left. You left me, yes, but at least I could look after myself. You left your paraplegic father alone in his unit. Yes, he has the basic care provided by paid services, but nothing else. After you departed, he didn't even leave his unit...'

Jamie dropped her arm and balled his fists at his side.

'For a while now, he's been part of some community groups, participates in outings, and sees people. Feels loved.'

'Sapphie, you have no idea.'

But now she was fuming mad. 'I have no idea? You left to pursue your own selfish dreams, and I took up your role. I care for your abandoned father. Someone has to. And if you aren't prepared to, I am.'

'No.'

'I understand you've changed. Have become a different person to the one I knew,' she paused, swallowed back the word, 'loved'. 'But when did you become heartless?' She stared him down and saw contrition in his face. But then it hardened; his eyes narrowed, and his shoulders drew back. Defying her, assuming she was wrong, or stupid or both.

'How do you sleep at night knowing what you've done?' The words were loaded and she didn't simply refer to his father, she referred to herself as well. Those words she never uttered, *How could you have left me when you said you loved me?* would probably always haunt her. Turning, she walked away.

The door breezed open and brought with it a gust of cool air. James frowned. It was early, too early for anyone else to be in the caverns of the factory yet. Though not a natural early riser, he had formed a habit of always arriving at work while the sun still climbed high above the surrounding mountain ranges. There was something to be said for the stillness that permeated the always bustling town at that hour, for the quietness that swallowed you, made you confront your thoughts and fears and gave you space to think.

The factory was always noisy with machines turning, conveyor belts running, voices chatting, packages being prepared, and paper rustling. There was something special when the world of chocolate production went quiet. Of course, he enjoyed it just as much in full throttle. It was such a thrill to see chocolates whizzing past and be so drowned in the taste and scent of chocolate that you thought you were chocolate. Precious.

So, he never expected anyone at this hour. His eyebrows shot to his forehead as he turned and saw Sapphire in the entrance to the kitchen, one hand still holding the door, preventing it from flinging back.

His frown disappeared and his body came alive. Until concern flooded through him. Sapphie's usual vibrancy was missing, her body appearing limp and heavy. 'What's wrong?'

She brightened immediately and scurried over, but he didn't buy it. 'Good morning,' she said, moving first to the corner where she placed Winnie's bed, now a permanent feature in that part of the kitchen, and released the dog who rushed towards him.

Winnie jumped in joy, and James crouched, jostling with her on the ground. 'Who's a beautiful girl, then?' he cooed, petting and stroking her when Winnie stood still. The love of a dog; he'd conveniently forgotten how loyal and caring they were. How with such little effort, they made you feel special.

Standing, he picked up Winnie and observed Sapphie.

Perhaps she was tired?

'Are you alright?'

Leaning against the bench, she sighed. 'I'm fine. A tiring weekend.'

Weekend? What had she got up to after Friday night?

Head bowed, she said, 'My family knows you are here. Are my mentor. I spent the entire weekend fielding calls from them and demanding me to return or for them to come here, getting them down off the proverbial ledge.'

Okay. No nights out on the town, then. He was pleased. But

then what she'd said registered. 'Sheesh, they hate me that much?'

'Nah, not so much, but they love me a lot. And are worried.'

'Did you explain I'm looking after you?'

The look on her face revealed her thoughts on that notion without words being necessary. 'Um, no. But it's fine. They just feel far away and aren't able to help if they need to.'

'Do you need their help?'

He saw the pause, her lips opened, then closed. 'No. Why would I?' Standing up taller, she looked around her. 'What are you doing here so early anyway?'

'I'm working.' Placing Winnie down, the dog immediately began exploring, no doubt hoping for a missed morsel or two of chocolate.

'What's so important at this hour?'

'It's for you, actually.' He paused for effect. Sapphie moved to gather her apron and wash her hands, ready for work. She never was a slacker. 'Any moment now, my old boss is arriving from London. The man who trained me after Seb, the man who changed my life. Seb taught me the basics, but Oliver taught me the art of chocolate-making and the business side of it, too.'

'Okay,' she said, 'but why's he coming?'

'To teach you.'

That made her pause. 'But I'm your student. You are my teacher.' She paused again as some sort of realisation spread across her face. 'You're upset with me about your dad, and now you won't teach me? Might as well send me home then. I'll let my family know.' And she moved to retrieve her mobile phone.

'That's not it.' He laced his fingers with hers, stilling her hand. Her skin was warm and smooth; he kept it there and looked up. Her gaze settled on their entwined fingers; within seconds, she wrenched it back, held it close to her side, rubbed her fingers where they'd connected.

He turned to face her and placed his hands on his hips. 'Listen, it's not about that.' She harrumphed and jostled on the spot. 'No, Sapphie, stop,' he reached for her arm, but quick as a whip, she tugged it out of reach. 'If you don't stop and listen, I'll keep touching you!'

The corners of her lips gave only the tiniest curl. 'I meant everything I said yesterday about you visiting my dad. There is stuff you don't understand and you must immediately stop visiting him. That's an order.'

Now she matched his stance with her hands on her hips, feet hip-width apart, a pugilist pose.

'Okay,' he held his hands up in surrender. 'Too heavy. I get it. It's my wish, then. Sound better?'

She didn't agree. Clearly, they were not going to get anywhere with that argument. But he had to, and he would. Not wanting to sound too dramatic about it, but it was a matter of life and death. He'd make her agree, but other matters first.

'You want to avoid me!' she accused.

'Don't be ridiculous,' he shot back.

'Yes, that's it.' Her head was nodding, convinced of her argument. 'Remember, I didn't set this whole stupid scenario up. I never asked to be tutored by you, to travel all this way . . . I . . . to see you again. It's not my fault you can't stand being with me, seeing me,' she bit her lip to suppress the sob. 'I need to learn new skills. I need to take back home as much knowledge as possible to help Seb and Hinterland Chocolate.'

'Sapphie, stop.' The word muffled as he embraced her, his

head resting atop hers. 'I had no idea you were that worried about the company. Of course, you'll take back new knowledge, which makes it even more important to learn from someone like Oliver. I'm not a teacher. He is wonderful and can show you so much more than me; wait and see.' His hug was fierce and tight, but Sapphire didn't fight it. Her body trembled in his embrace.

'Oliver is one of the best chocolatiers in Europe.'

'So are you,' she interrupted, her voice breaking.

He couldn't help his grin. 'Thank you, I do happen to agree. But maybe it's best you are guided by someone else...'

'Someone else?' she questioned.

'Someone who isn't me?'

She drank in his words, pulled out of his embrace and gazed at him until she was distracted by Winnie sniffing around the floor, but he thought he saw a barely discernible nod.

'The two weeks is almost up anyway. I'll go home at the end of it.' She uttered the words without looking at him. He was formulating his reply when the door flung back once more.

'James!' A strong, robust voice sang out and a big presence entered the room.

'Oliver.' James rushed over and back-slapped the giant of a man.

Chapter Nineteen

I t was like Santa Claus himself had entered the kitchen. It was a great distraction. Sapphire had too many thoughts bubbling around in her brain, and she didn't know what to think. Jamie wanted to spend time with her. Jamie didn't want to spend time with her. She was better mentored by someone else. But he was her teacher. She was here for him. The cries of despair from her family rang out in her head . . . and well, damn it, she was confused. So, the arrival of the oafish man with his white hair and white beard was timely. Each word he uttered was loud, and his presence took up the entire room. How on earth was she going to work with this fellow? After their greetings, Oliver approached her. En route, Winnie sprang out of nowhere and leapt at his legs. The man emitted the most raucous laugh; Sapphire couldn't do anything but giggle along with it.

Clearly, no one was immune to the dog's charm. The white fluff ball enamoured everyone in her path, even big, tough men, it would appear.

Eventually, he made it to her. He grasped her two hands in his, lifted her left hand to his lips, and kissed it. It was a very European grand gesture, but the accent escaping his mouth was anything but. Cockney English at its best.

'You're English!' she exclaimed, and laughter erupted between them, releasing the tension, well, her tension, anyway.

'Yes, and why does that surprise you?' Oliver asked in return with a broad grin.

'I'm so sorry, Jamie didn't say, and I simply assumed someone who has the accolades of being one of the best choco-latiers in Europe would be German or Swiss.'

Oliver did a double take between them. 'Jamie, hey?' he jested and joined in the

revelry. 'Sorry to disappoint you, my dear, but I belong to the Motherland. Even though I am always happy to visit the continent, especially when my protégés are doing so well.' He patted Jamie on the back in a fatherly fashion. She observed the two men who had obvious affection for one another.

'Dinner tonight, my friend, we must catch up. But I have a day's work to do first, and most importantly, you are to spend time with a new protégée. Dare I say, she's better than me? I was a good student, could apply anything I was taught, but Sapphie is a natural talent.'

Warmth flushed her neck and cheeks, and she hoped she wasn't bright red.

'Is that right?' Oliver mused. 'There may be nothing left to teach you.' Glancing around the kitchen, he asked, 'Will we be working here today?'

Jamie nodded agreement.

'Okay, it looks well kitted out, thank you. What about

recipes, James, information, or at the very least a product list? Are we to practise on your range?'

'You hardly need recipes, Oliver,' Jamie avoided the man's eye and became suddenly fixated on Winnie.

'James.' The word was forceful and required attention. It worked, and Jamie stopped fidgeting and stared directly. 'Please, James, this can't continue.' Heavy silence hung in the air.

'James, it's me. You can trust me. We've known each other a long time now, haven't we? I thought, hoped maybe, that by you inviting me out here, you'd relaxed your stringent rules about sharing knowledge, details, well, sharing anything. I'd hoped perhaps that you had learned not to be so secretive.'

Sapphire observed the exchange. Jamie remained silent.

'What's happened to you in the past that you don't trust anyone?' Oliver's words were gentle and tender, someone who cared.

Sapphire's head snapped up. Trust anyone? What was he talking about? She cast her mind rapidly back, rewinding time, but nothing appeared in her memory bank. Jamie had always been open and honest with her; they'd shared their hopes dreams, and ideas for the future. He'd been a valuable member of the Hinterland team.

Until he wasn't.

His leaving had been all kinds of strange. A shock. Sudden. Not just to her but to everyone they knew in the small community and his workmates. One day, they'd shared their future; the next, he was leaving Canungra, pursuing his dreams overseas, and alone, without her. His leaving was a flurry of pain, hurt, and disbelief. He'd gone from being loving, her everything, to cold and distant overnight.

Had something happened? And if yes, what?

Jamie recovered his power of speech and spoke to his friend. 'Oliver, you are well aware that this is a lucrative business, cut-throat, particularly here on the continent; you can't trust anyone!'

Oliver shook his head. 'My friend, it is a business, one that we all want to be the best in, to succeed by having the top sales and most sought-after contracts, the best chocolate. But you forget, chocolate is chocolate. It is made the same way. Yes, if we are lucky, we might invent a combination of new flavours that everyone adores and tops the sales charts, become the next big thing, but hey, there are so many options—'

Jamie interrupted. 'Of course, the base recipe of chocolate is the same; I'm not stupid. But if I tell you who I supply my chocolates to, won't you want to work harder to secure a deal with them instead of me? Won't you want to come here and discover what new ideas we have? Of the innovations we might be exploring? Of the advertising we are implementing? Of the way we run our office?'

'Anyone ethical in business would never steal ideas or copy their competitor. It is about being original, yes?'

Jamie's mobile phone rang, ending the conversation. He answered and moved away to discuss whatever it was with the person on the phone, reinforcing that whatever Oliver said was not agreed.

Oliver turned towards her, his smile broad and wide, filling his face. 'Let's get started, my dear.'

Sapphire didn't understand or know what had transpired and what the confrontation between two of the best choco-latiers in Europe meant, but she was only here for one thing—

the chocolate. A frisson of excitement passed through her. It wasn't lost on her that she was being given a wonderful opportunity, and she planned on sucking Oliver dry of his secrets. If Jamie, wouldn't share, it sounded like Oliver would.

That afternoon, James walked the length of the village and back, and his anger still flared. Admittedly, it wasn't far enough to cool the hot flash of rage that sat in his chest, ready to burst and spew vitriol.

Arriving at the cottage, he heard Winnie barking and stormed around the back. Sapphire lay on the verdant grass, Winnie zooming around her with speed. Occasionally, the dog paused, and Sapphie tried to scoop her up, only for her to whizz away and for the game to continue.

Sapphire giggled, something he hadn't enjoyed much of during her time in Hallstatt. But there was nothing to chuckle about today.

'Have you read this?' He shoved the newspaper into her line of vision. Winnie got wind of his presence and immediately weaved around his legs, jumping in excitement and barking. James shoved the dog down, and she scuttled away to seek protection beside Sapphire, who now sat up.

With one hand blocking the glorious afternoon sun, she read the paper. 'Um, no. The newspaper is in German.'

He snatched it back and turned the page over, thrusting the half-page photograph into her face. There was no need for translation to understand what she saw.

'What, what is this?' she spluttered, sitting up straighter now on the grass, ignoring the dog. Something twisted inside him at the sound of her words. Surprise? Shock? A twinge of doubt gripped him, but just as quickly, he shook it off.

'Let me translate.' And he read the article that went into great detail about the previous relationship between the mysterious new mentee of the Grindelwald chocolate brand and its new owner. After exhausting their past, it described the nature of their relationship now, added in a large dose of innuendo about the choice of mentee given their past status and listed things they'd done together since her arrival, including skiing in Zermatt. There was one large photograph, recent and from one of the thousands taken for their social media publicity and then a collection of smaller, curated images that, at first glance, appeared to be intimate, of them standing close together mixing chocolate, of them smiling at each other in the kitchen, playing with Winnie.

'But the clincher,' James paused, and by now Sapphire was on her feet, her brow furrowed with deep crevices while Winnie was ignored and racing around the small terrace yard, 'is that they can reveal news of an exciting new range of products to be released before Christmas.' He paused for dramatic effect and lowered the paper, 'the range that no one knows about.' Then he scrunched the paper up into a ball and held it in his clenched fist.

'Including me,' she said her voice tiny, barely there.

'It's interesting, isn't it,' his voice rising in intonation, 'that these facts are only known to you and me, and I haven't spoken to any journalists of the local weekend paper with its glossy magazine insert—'

'Hang on, neither have I! You think I told them these . . .

these private details? I revealed that we were once an item. I did not,' she shook her head, and her blonde bob moved with each turn, strands getting stuck in her mouth, 'and plus, I don't know anything about your new range. How could I? You never tell me anything, and everything around you is top secret!'

'And yet Marie and Jakob tell me you're at the factory early *every* morning,' he emphasised the word, 'that's plenty of time to snoop around and find out stuff.'

The look she gave him he'd seen only once before. When he'd told her he was leaving. . .Back then, he'd had to leave and get out of the Gold Coast fast to avoid that look, but now, he was simply raving mad that she could betray him.

And like last time, he watched the anger, indignation, and hurt, with lack of understanding, seep away, and Sapphire admit defeat, like a dog in submission, giving up and rolling onto its back.

Despite her body language, her tone was clear, cutting like steel. 'You think I'd embarrass myself by telling the story of our past to the world? That I would reveal that the man I loved more than anything, the man I had a future with, a man I shared dreams and hopes with, left me without a proper explanation and moved across the world to pursue his chocolate-making career? That after reluctantly signing your confidentiality agreement, I would breach it by telling people outside of the factory your secrets and personal information. That I would sneak into your factory early and, what was your word, snoop for secret intel, and then sell it to the paper? *James.*' His full name on her lips sounded exaggerated and vindictive, improper, nasty. 'You are wrong. That's the difference between us. I would never do that. I would never sell out those close to me, those dear to me, those I loved, unlike you.'

Winnie sniffed her leg, demanding attention. She scooped up the small white dog and held her close to her cheek, taking comfort in her soft fur. 'Oliver is obviously right. Something has happened to you; something has changed you. You would never have behaved like you are, once, before,' she flashed one arm around, 'all hoity toity and rich and better than anyone else. Acting as if people care about what you do, how you make the chocolate, flying around in your fancy jet . . .I am so mad at myself. So angry that I pined for you. I pined for the man I loved who left me. But that man no longer exists. That man may never have existed. Perhaps he was a figment of my imagination. Or perhaps that is who you are and you were biding your time until you had enough skills to master the world of chocolate-making. Maybe we were convenient, maybe you used us all. But I am not like you. I am honest and sincere, and I am not a liar or a cheat. I have not spoken to any journalists, and I will never. I will protect the dastardly things you did to me and . . . you know what? Maybe you've done me a favour. Bringing me here, opening my eyes. I know what's important and what matters to me, and you know what, thank goodness, that's no longer you.'

She moved away, and he jerked an arm out to grasp her wrist. 'You might hate me and I don't blame you, but you are wasting your life. Oliver agrees with me; you are a naturally talented chocolatier. You are underutilised at Hinterland. You could work anywhere, you could work with Oliver in England, be involved in some of the best chocolate productions in the world, make chocolate like you've never made before, and be something, become someone. Can't you see how good you are? You are committing yourself to being a nothing, a nobody, a choco-latier no one has ever heard of. If nothing else from this trip, realise your potential, chase your dreams, do something!'

Sapphire released a sob and covered her mouth as if annoyed her body betrayed her. Head bowed, she went to the back door of the cabin and slammed it shut hard, the sound reverberating around the terrace and through each inch of his body.

It was the most Sapphie had ever said. The clearest and most demanding she'd ever voiced her opinion. She'd pined for him? Like he had missed her? She didn't understand, could never understand . . .

But the article revealed his secrets and their private past; it had to be her. No one else knew. She was the only person in possession of that information. And yes, she hadn't had any idea about the new Christmas range, but it was super easy to find out. That twinge of doubt returned. It demanded attention, became stronger, more forceful, and squeezed his heart too tight, as if it were being squashed in a vice.

Chapter Twenty

'Marcus, where's Lina? I need to speak to her.'

Sapphire entered the offices of Grindelwald, perhaps for the last time. Despite her best efforts at face creams and rinses, her eyes remained red-rimmed and puffy after a sleepless night.

She was a nobody?

She was nothing? Wasting her life? And moreover, apparently a liar.

Well, she'd show James White. He might consider her a nothing, but she'd go home and happily be a simple chocolate maker for the Australian people, work hard and serve her employer, and be an important part of their world and of her family, of course. There were different definitions of success.

His words kept niggling at her, though, like an annoying mosquito bite, no, the worst case of hives you could ever have. But that wouldn't stop her; she'd made up her mind about what came next, and now she needed Lina's help to set her plan in motion.

Marcus looked around him and leaned in close. 'She's not here, and I can't find her.' Pointing to her desk, he said, 'and her desk is cleaned out. I mean, tidy, everything personal gone.' He waited as if expecting Sapphire to hold the answers.

'She's gone? What, I mean, where? How? Why?'

'Clearly, you know no more than I do. Lina didn't speak to you? Tell you anything?'

'I haven't seen her since our day taking photographs and the drinks afterwards. Have you?'

'Oh, yeah, sure, but she didn't say anything.'

'I'm sure she'll be back.' But Sapphire wasn't sure of any such thing. Lina gone? The integral part of Grindelwald's PR team missing, AWOL, absconded? It didn't make sense. But she had too much else to worry about.

'Well, okay, I need your help then. I need to change my flight details. I'm heading home.'

'Home? What?' He reached out and gripped her wrist, his face filled with anguish. 'No, you can't. I'm not sure what's going on here, but you can't leave too. No. That's not the PR plan.'

Sapphire shook her head. 'I know the original plan. But Jamie promised that if I wanted to go after two weeks, he'd permit it. It's been two weeks and now I'm asking to go home. Can you arrange it?'

'Sapphire, I can't. I don't have the authority. You know that Lina ran this team, the publicity, this campaign. She called the shots...'

'But she's not here...'

'Y-e-s, and without her, the man in charge is the boss. She was answerable to James.'

That stopped her in her tracks. Ask Jamie to change her flight details? She never wanted to speak to the man again. In fact, she wanted to erase any memory or thought of him from her past, her present, and her future. Act and feel like he'd never existed. So, asking him for help was out of the question. Not Marcus's problem, though. She placed one hand over his and patted in a comforting gesture. 'I'm sure everything will work out. Lina was devoted to this job, there's a reason, I'm sure.' Marcus did not look convinced. 'Or maybe you'll get a promotion?' Sapphire shrugged. 'But if I don't see you again, thank you for your kindness. Collecting me when I first arrived, making me welcome. Being funny.'

Marcus relaxed and broke out into a smile. 'I still insist you aren't going...but my first Australian. You were a treasure, Sapphire Banks, and don't let anyone tell you otherwise.' They kissed on the cheek, and she waved goodbye.

Sapphire deposited Winnie into the safety of the kitchen. Despite her love for the dog, she'd never dream of taking her into the working confines of the warehouse. The hygiene and scandal; if anyone knew a dog had been in the sacred chocolate-making space, she'd never risk it.

Weaving her way through the rooms, she waved to everyone and addressed them by their first name. It hadn't taken long to get to know the staff. Each day in the factory would do that. But she had one purpose for now, and that was to find Marie and Jakob. Today, they worked together on the end of the Turkish delight conveyor, inspecting the covered jellies at the conclusion of their journey before being packaged. Their sweet smell was intoxicating.

'I have a huge favour to ask,' she said to Marie as she sidled up next to her. 'I'm heading home soon, and I'm wondering whether you'll care for Winnie at night? It's perfect because she can become the factory mascot during the day; she's very used to it now. But she can't stay here alone at night. Can you take her home each evening?'

'You're leaving?' Jakob intervened.

'It was only ever temporary, and now, well, it's time. I've learned so much in the last two weeks. Enough for a lifetime. I need to take that knowledge home now.'

Together, they expressed their thanks and gratitude for helping them and for becoming part of the Grindelwald family. 'And, James, of course, he is aware that Winnie will stay?'

Sheesh, why did everything come back to *James*? It had always been her intention to leave Winnie in his care. She knew once he'd become accustomed to the dog and began to love her, he'd never abandon her, and perhaps, leaving her in the factory, that might still happen. Crossing her fingers behind her back, she hoped so. But for now, she stared her new friends in the eyes. 'Yes, he's aware.' Her face was deadpan and serious, her crossed fingers no doubt turning white, as she held them tight.

They hugged once more. 'I have my last lesson with Oliver, then I'll be off.' It had been such a short friendship, and Marie and Jakob were old enough to be her parents, but she'd enjoyed getting to know them. Like her, they loved chocolate and were committed and devoted to its production. A surge of affection for the pair passed through her, and she hoped their paths might cross again one day.

Without turning back, she headed towards the kitchen. Entering, she saw Oliver playing with Winnie. Her heart lurched into her throat. Leaving that dog was going to be hard, and the prospect of it made her nauseous.

'Ah, here she is, Winnie, the star of the show.'

'Stop it, Oliver,' she said playfully. 'I can't thank you enough for your lessons. You've been brilliant, so calm, and so knowledgeable. I have learned so much; I'm truly grateful.'

'You are very welcome. It is such a joy to share the passion with someone. And you have that. You cannot fake the passion for chocolate, the love. It is our first love.'

'Oliver, you know, I'd work for you in a heartbeat if your business was in Australia because you represent everything I love about this industry when it's done ethically and morally, and we can make wonderful products, but not at the cost of the lives of those that supply the beans and farm for us. You do it properly even though it's the more difficult path, but you show everyone else it's possible.'

'Thank you, cherub. I would dearly love to have you working with me, not for me. That offer remains open always. You remember that. But I understand and appreciate your pull for home. It is the same for me. I could be living here on the continent, but my life is in England, where I was born and raised. I love it there, like you love your family and your life in Australia. I understand. But I was thinking a bit more about your factory. I will visit it one day, but let me share more about what I did to make ethical chocolate successful. The first thing to remember is that it's a long game. It is hard to change people's perceptions, and sometimes they are simply unaware of the circumstances behind the production of chocolate, and other times, people don't want to know.'

Oliver kept her enthralled for the next hour with tips and tricks to manage an ethical chocolate-making business with moral practices and higher prices. The biggest recommendation was to make their business international. And that didn't mean moving the factory, but in this current environment of a global world, it had never been easier to advertise, sell and ship products. He also mentioned international Expos and fairs as a great way to get their name out there in a competitive and busy market.

'Now, let's make one last thing together. Something special and memorable.'

―――――――――

Back in the cabin, hours later, Sapphire captured each room, the view, the terrace, and each nook and cranny on her phone. She wanted to remember everything about this place. When would she ever again gaze out a window and see snow-capped mountain ranges within a hair's breadth, as if she could reach those tough and rough textures with her fingertips? Hallstatt sure was one heck of a place. From the beauty and expanse of its lake to the mountain ranges surrounding it and the village hugging it, the quaint shops, the people, and the food. She had experienced an entire lifetime in only a few short weeks.

And of course, Jamie.

Just two short weeks ago, she'd spent most of her days pining for her lost love, the man she adored, the man she still loved. Flying across the world, she'd found him. But it wasn't the fairy-tale ending. Because she hadn't found him, her previous love, the man she'd wanted to spend the rest of her life with. He'd been replaced by a rich, upper-class, high-flying chocolatier. She couldn't blame him for the chocolate part. That was always their shared dream: to be successful chocolatiers. However, it was a dream to share at home at Hinterland. He'd become a first-class chocolatier by travelling the world and learning from some of the best. Warmth spread across her chest at the thought of Oliver. What a wonderful influence on Jamie, but it hadn't seemed to make a difference.

People changed, she guessed. And she had, too, in only these short weeks. Just as Jamie had, it would be hard to remain the same after the exposure he'd had to things. It had to change a person.

What! No. No defending him. One thing she'd learned is that it had to be about her now, even though it still hurt. The pain remained real, and the anguish was sometimes unbearable. But she'd work hard to push that aside, knowing that Jamie no longer existed and James now took his place. James was not who she loved. He was a different man. So hard though, when there were glimpses of the man she loved underneath on occasion, when he sometimes let his guard down. Gone was the fun-loving, sincere and loyal man; in his place was a guarded, serious and uptight fellow.

Plus, the nerve of him accusing her of revealing their past! That was a low blow and unforgivable. Didn't he know her at all?

She hadn't come for closure, but she'd got it. Jamie had forged a new life, a life without her and it was time for her to go home and reinvent herself, whoever that was. The bangle at her wrist was smooth and cool, comforting. It always had been, but also a clutch, a dream. It helped keep the ridiculous idea alive that Jamie might come back for her and that he might still love her. She knew better now. Twirling the thick gold for the last time, she removed it, ran both sets of fingers around it, and felt its curves, smooth edges, the clasp. The tears couldn't be held at bay this time as she let the bracelet rest on the timber table in the dining room. It sat alone, bereft, like her.

Chapter Twenty-One

Multiple light bulbs flashed, blinding him despite his Versace sunglasses, and a stampede of people rushed towards him. Questions were shouted, and bodies pushed and shoved to get close. The menagerie of people talking all at once caused the words to become garbled. Instinctively, James held up his Italian leather briefcase in front of him as a shield.

For the briefest of moments, he was chuffed. Being human, it was hard not to be complimented by folks wanting your photograph and to capture your every spoken word, but the first shove to his back made that sentiment disappear faster than a deflating balloon.

He struggled with each step forward but could see the entrance to the factory. He was close. Shoving away the cluster of mics pushed into his face, he tried to control his rising temper. There was a reason he avoided the media.

'Is it true you fled Australia and your position as chocolatier in disgrace?' Someone yelled from the back.

He mis stepped, and his expression must have given away his surprise as the group grew quiet, holding their breath, waiting for a scoop, hoping they were onto something big.

'What can you tell us about your relationship with your mentee?'

'When was the last time you saw your family?'

'What does Hinterland Chocolate think about your success?'

He hung his head, eyes downcast; thoughts rushed into his mind so fast he couldn't catch them. Where did these comments come from?

The newspaper article.

'If you won't answer those questions, can you tell us about your Christmas special?'

He was pulled up short for the second time. His pulse slowed as they progressed onto safer topics. Or were they?

Where the hell was Lina? She needed to be out here on the hustings, answering these questions with aplomb while also giving as little away as possible. Or perhaps not, as the throng continued to shout, trying to be heard above each other.

He had the entire Christmas collection catalogued and pictured in a glossy brochure locked in his desk drawer. He could recite it from memory, each glorious artisan piece. Should he give them a morsel? Whet their appetite? He paused, head raised, held high and moved forward again before pausing, uncertain. His head told him to keep quiet. This was a trap. Reveal nothing. Or was he wrong? One mention in an article and this was the response? Mind-blowing. Spare of the moment, he made a decision.

He passed his case to the colleague next to him, pulled on his jacket sleeves, evened his cuff links and wiped his hands down his front. 'We will be releasing the range on October 15th.' Notepads were pulled from pockets, and pencils scribbled furiously.

'Can you give us a hint of what customers can expect?'

'Something different to our usual star range.' And he turned on his heel and left them behind, talking on mobile phones, taking photographs of his departing back, and muttering amongst themselves.

Inside, the phones rang. His front receptionist was frazzled: she answered one call and placed another on hold whilst commandeering the people loitering in the foyer. With hands uplifted in the measure of defeat, she kept talking into the phone.

'Ma'am, can I help you?' James asked the lady at the front of the queue.

'Oh, Fred,' she elbowed the man next to her, 'it's Mr White himself.' She fluffed up her hair a little and then offered her hand to shake. 'So lovely to meet you. The people of Hallstatt are so happy with how things are going with the factory. You've put the brand and our town, back on the map, so to speak.'

He thanked her and enquired again whether she wanted to make a purchase and if she should perhaps be heading towards the shop, where he kindly pointed in the right direction to guide her.

'No, well, yes. I wanted to order the Christmas specials. I don't want to miss out.'

Spinning on the spot, he clapped his hands together and shushed the crowd. 'Good morning, everyone; I'm James White, local manager of Grindelwald. Are you all here to order the Christmas special?'

It was unanimous. 'Well, that's wonderful. I can't thank you enough for your interest and your support. I'm delighted, but unfortunately, it isn't available yet. We are releasing the catalogue for orders in the middle of next month, plenty of time for Christmas.' Shoulders drooped, and there was a collective sigh of disappointment.

Finger to his chin, he thought quickly. 'But I tell you what, as a measure of your goodwill and for showing such interest and turning up today, if you leave your name and details,' and he walked behind the desk and extracted a yellow A4 pad, 'on here, I will ensure that each of you will be dispatched the first orders and, as an added bonus, we'll include another something special with your delivery, and that is only for you good folk here today.'

A collective cheer went up, and people bustled to get to the front of the line.

Acting out of character and feeling quite discombobulated, he continued. 'And for everyone, there's free chocolate!' He literally reached into the various barrels lining the walls of the foyer and threw handfuls of goodies into the air. People scrabbled. Apologetically, he left his capable receptionist to it and backed out of the room, taking the internal stairs two at a time.

'Lina,' he yelled, entering the offices upstairs. Marcus was on the phone, nodding, noting down something. He caught the words *Vogue, Vanity Fair* and *Time*.

Swivelling on a chair with wheels, he waited until Marcus hung up.

'Wow, this is incredible, but also disturbing.' His words were almost inaudible. James shoved his fringe off his face, even though his hair barely touched his forehead.

'Where did they come from, and why are they here?' His face was a patchwork of creases.

Marcus slapped him on the back, oblivious to his inner turmoil. 'That was *Vogue* wanting an exclusive with you, a full interview and photo shoot and I've already received messages from *Time* Magazine and *Style*!'

The chair crashed against the desk.

'I know right? This is seriously freaking awesome.'

'But where is Lina? I need her to help me deal with the masses, say those catchphrases she's so good at, and take shots for our channel and pages. Where is she? She needs to field those calls you're taking and tell them I'm not interested.' He swivelled on the chair once more.

'W-e-l-l,' Marcus dragged out the syllables, 'she's not here.' He cast a furtive glance at her desk in the corner, and James's eyes followed. He got up swiftly, paused in front of the bare desk and brushed his hand across the clean top.

'I don't understand.'

'Yeah, me neither, boss. But here's something strange: there's a message from the paper that ran the spread on you, and they want to chat to Lina *again*.' Marcus let the silence hang.

'*Again*? As in she's spoken to them before?'

'Mmm, and there's more.' Marcus uncoded his phone, swiped across pages, and held up the screen for James to see.

'No.' It came out as a groan and he snatched at the phone as if getting up closer to the image might change it. In front of him was an image of Lina holding a basket of their competitor's chocolates and standing in front of their impressive head office in Germany. His gut twisted. It couldn't be happening again, could it? Not twice. Once was impossible to accept, difficult to forget, but twice?

No, but then reality crashed down upon him, like the ceiling falling in, with a sudden thwack to his back. No. No. He'd be okay; his company would be okay. Since last time, he'd kept his mouth shut, never revealing even the slightest detail for others to absorb, use, copy, steal, or sell. It was the one thing he was absolutely sure of. In fact, this morning was the most detail he'd ever given about the company and its products, which hadn't been publicly available since his arrival only months ago.

But then, outside, there'd been that question. About before; home. No one knew about his past. The only information had been in that article. Now, people were asking about it; those journalists were probably digging up the dirt, and his history had rushed forward . . . since Sapphire arrived.

And now Lina had defected to their largest competitor?

Oliver entered the room. 'James, what is it? What's happened?' His friend approached; his face etched with concern. The back of James' throat ached with the taste of bile, and his body temperature rose, so he tugged at the tie restricting his neck.

James needed a brandy, but with the clock not yet struck midday, he'd have to settle for a hot chocolate. Together he and Oliver sat drinking, both quiet, deep in thought. Until the door crashed back against the frame, and Marcus entered his office without knocking.

'It's true, boss. I spoke with *Das Tagliche*, *The Daily*, and they confirmed the only source for the article in the paper was Lina. She wasn't even a secret source, so they were happy to divulge her name.'

'They didn't speak to Sapphire?' he enquired.

'No.'

Oliver spoke up then. 'You thought Sapphire leaked news of your past and of the business to the paper?'

'Thank you, Marcus,' James said and waited for him to exit.

'Sapphire was the only person who knew about our relationship, about my past, our history. So, of course, I presumed she was the leak. I honestly don't know how Lina knew those details.'

'You and Sapphire...?' Oliver probed.

James took a sip of his drink, still wishing it had a drop of something stronger in it. 'Sapphire and I, we were a thing.' *A thing*? He was pathetic. 'We dated and had plans. We were serious, were engaged to marry and had planned a future together.'

Oliver offered a deep 'hmmm.'

'What does that mean?' Jamie continued when his friend didn't reply. 'I was the head chocolatier at Hinterland and Sapphire joined the team and raced up the ranks. She was good, as you know. We were both trained by the head chocolatier at the time, and I took over from him. Sapphire worked with me, and then, well, we fell in love.

'We had it all worked out. We would marry, run the factory eventually and spend our lives together making chocolate.' He smiled, rueful and full of memory. 'I loved her.'

Oliver's stare was penetrating, but he remained silent.

'My mother died giving birth to me. I have always lived with my father. Quite a few years ago, he was injured in a car accident and became a paraplegic, confined to a wheelchair.' Oliver placed his hand over his. The gesture almost broke him, and sobs desperately tried to escape his chest.

'I became his primary carer. That was fine. We lived in a simple unit but had it modified for his chair, and I worked hard to provide for him. I thought we were doing okay, but he, I guess, found things difficult . . .'

'I can imagine . . .' Oliver commented.

'He commenced drinking a lot, trying to forget what life might have been, I guess, perhaps wishing for a different future. I tried to do my best. But he continued to drink. Then I noticed expensive items like wagyu steak for dinner, then he'd have a new fancy watch and other items I hadn't bought for him, and we couldn't afford. It came to a head, and he admitted...' James' voice cracked. 'He confessed that he'd been selling the trade secrets and information I'd been telling him about the chocolate factory. I thought we were casually chatting!' James became more animated at the memory of it. Angry. Furious. 'Because he didn't do much, after I'd finished work for the day, I'd come home, and we'd talk. He showed a lot of interest in the factory and what we were doing, and planning, and I'd tell him.'

James sat up straight, eyes glistening, and looked directly at Oliver. 'Yeah, he took great interest. He paid too much attention and then sold that information to the factory's competitor. Sold customer lists, recipes, and product information, anything and everything he could find out. I was absolutely gutted. Devastated. The company was my family and to have my father betray me and them, well.' James hung his head.

'I thought it couldn't get any worse. But when I forced my father to stop profiting from the information of the company, the guy, a rather unattractive sort, as you can imagine, threatened me. He said if the arrangement didn't continue, he'd reveal everything. That I was the one selling the secrets, performing insider trading, basically. Do you know the penalty for that crime? A hefty fine and jail time. Plus, the embarrassment. I couldn't contemplate it. I paid him off; it cost me a fortune, and I fled. Like a child, I fled the country, away from the scene of the crime, to forget and put it all behind me. But more importantly, to remove myself. If I wasn't there feeding my father information, there was nothing to tell.' He paused and gathered himself. 'Then I had to work damn hard to make back the money, and quickly, I was broke, my father needed money for his care . . . and so I worked hard,' he spread his hands wide, 'and here I am. Rich and successful and still running from the past.'

'That's terrible, James. I'm so sorry that happened to you. And that was when you came to England, to me. But you left Sapphire behind. Did you tell her?'

He shook his head. 'I was so embarrassed and angry that my father had put me in that position. That the company that had taught me everything I knew, made me the chocolatier I was, suffered because of me. I could no longer trust my father, could no longer work for them to provide him with any information to sell. I thought if I removed myself, things would work themselves out; the company would be okay, and they'd continue and prosper without me.'

'I guess I understand that. Even though I'm sure if you had

to defend yourself, the company would have understood and would have stood by you. You weren't even the one giving away the information!'

'I know, but it felt like a risk I couldn't take.'

'And Sapphire was the collateral damage?'

'Yeah. I haven't seen her since I left, that is until she turned up here. It brought everything back, and then suddenly, out of nowhere, my past is thrown in my face, the paper is writing about it, people asking questions.'

'Do you think you can run from this forever? Forget that it happened?' James digested this. 'What your father did was rotten, unfair and wrong and put you in an untenable position.'

'Saying anything would have implicated my father, put him in the spotlight, revealed that he was a cheat, a liar who had committed a crime. It was, is, a small country community. He would have been vilified.'

'Yes.'

'What? What are you not saying?'

'Sapphire is a great girl. I've seen you together. She adores you.'

'She hates me.'

'She wants to hate you, and I've seen her try hard to do that. But underneath,' he shrugged, 'I suspect she feels differently. You also did a terrible thing, not being honest with her, fleeing when she thought you had a future together. It must have been rough.'

'You don't need to rub it in. I acted abominably.'

'Perhaps it's time to make amends.'

'What? Tell her the truth? She's been visiting my father, is friends with him, thinks he's great. This will crumble her world.'

'You've already done that.'

The friends stared at each other in silence for moments until Oliver spoke. 'Now it might be time to stop running from your past. Be honest. Clear your conscience. You did nothing wrong to the company. Your father did. Then you acted poorly by running away. But perhaps it's time to fix the past. Or at least apologise for your part. She may not forgive you, but it's worth a shot. Perhaps if you clear the air with her, you can forge a better future, one where you can break down some barriers, let people in, trust them. Not everyone is like your father.'

Winnie wandered into his office and James scooped low and picked her up. He was reminded of how much Sapphie loved this dog, how much she loved their dog, Winston, and how much she loved him. Hang on, Winnie was here at the factory, alone, where was Sapphie?

'Did you have your lesson with Sapphire today?'

'Yes, our last session, this morning. We chatted about lots of things, more so than baking.'

'Have you seen her since?'

'No, but have you checked the kitchen or the factory? She's often wandering around.'

James's heart leapt into his throat. For the past two weeks, Sapphie had been a permanent fixture at the factory, unless she was with him. And in the last week, she and Winnie had been together, always. Something wasn't right. He rose quickly and then sat again.

'I should talk to her.' It was a statement but sounded more like a question.

'Yes, James, it's time to do the right thing. Face your past.

You are a world-class chocolatier, a smart man. Fix things and clear your conscience. Do you love her?'

No hesitation. 'I've always loved her.'

He patted him on the back and said, 'Go, my friend.'

Had he stuffed things up twice? Had he had a chance to fix things and not taken advantage of it? What an idiot he'd been! And blind.

Sapphie had been right in front of him for two weeks! The weight he'd carried at being around her all that time and continuing to carry his secret suddenly lifted at the thought of unadulterated redemption.

Flying as fast as his legs would carry him, he arrived at the cabin and banged on the door before calming himself down. Frightening Sapphie was not his intention. He rapped more quietly and waited, bouncing on his toes. It was time; it felt right to do this now, after all this time. Time to be honest. Face the music, he guessed.

There was no answer. He turned the doorknob and it released. 'Sapphie?' he called out. The cabin was quiet and a sense of dread deposited itself in his stomach.

Traversing the cabin from front to back and again, he discovered she wasn't there. The closest was empty, her bags gone; she was gone. Slumping onto the sofa, his mind went blank. He hadn't thought past seeing her, confessing, being honest. Now, he'd been robbed of the chance because he'd taken too long to come to his senses. Then he saw it. A glint of gold shone in the rays of sun streaming into the room.

The band of gold sat alone on the timber dining table. The bangle that Sapphie never took off, and had worn since the day he gave it to her, was here, without her. Picking it up, he went to throw it across the room but stopped himself in time. He wrapped it in a tissue and deposited it safely into his back pocket. Then he slammed his fist against the timber top and growled. If he'd thought he'd stuffed up already, this simply confirmed it. Sapphie had truly given up on him now. And this time, she'd fled and left him behind.

Chapter Twenty-Two

'I wasn't sure I'd see you again.'

'What? Why? I was always coming back.' Sapphire walked over to the man in the wheelchair and kissed his cheek. 'It's lovely to see you.' After the kiss, she commenced unpacking her full canvas carry bag. 'Today, I've brought Hinterland chocolate, of course, homemade jam drops, and some fudge from the store in town.' She placed the produce on the small corner table.

Michael watched her as she faffed about plumping cushions, collecting bottles and cans for the recycle bin, and putting the kettle on for a cuppa. When she re-entered the living room holding two steaming mugs of tea, he waited as she plonked herself in the sofa chair. 'So he didn't tell you then?'

'What? Who?'

'It's all-around town that your secret mentor was Jamie.'

Sapphire sipped her tea and stalled for time. 'Yeah, but it wasn't a secret. Well, it wasn't meant to be, but as it turned out, it was him. Even Seb didn't realise, and after the shock wore off,

I didn't want my family to worry. But when they found out, there was little chance of my having to break the news to anyone else after they blabbed it around town to everyone they saw. He sends his regards.'

'He does not,' Michael replied.

'What happened between you two?' she asked, cupping her mug for warmth.

'After all this time, I'm puzzled he didn't tell you. I don't know whether to be chuffed he's protecting me or troubled that he's still running from the past.'

Sapphire was shaking her head. 'I'm not following.'

Michael glanced around the room, sipped his tea, and took his time. 'Jamie left because of me.'

Her head was shaking before she replied. 'He left because he saw an opportunity he wanted to seize. A chance to become bigger and better than the rest of us and a chocolatier of the world.' Her words dripped in sarcasm.

'That's not true, Sapphire. The boy loved you, truly loved you. He was honest and genuine and worked hard, and saw a future with you.'

Then he started and didn't stop. Sapphire placed her cup onto the coffee table, not trusting herself to avoid spilling the hot contents into her lap, and settled back to listen to Michael tell the story. At times, her mouth was agape; other times, her head hung low, barely able to look him in the eye.

'You deserve the truth.'

'Yes, but clearly not enough that Jamie thought he could tell me himself.' Her thoughts were in a spiral. Did he still love her? Had he always loved her? Could they be together?

Well, obviously not. If he couldn't tell her what had

happened when they were thrown together five years later in unexpected circumstances, then there was probably little chance he ever would. He'd obviously decided to forge a new life, a life as a chocolatier in Europe, thoughts of her, of their previous dreams, forgotten. It reinforced that she had to do the same. Instinctively, she reached for the bangle to find her wrist bare. It had been such a wrench taking it off—the final conclusion of a chapter she knew had to end, but she was still convincing herself.

'Thank you for telling me.'

'I am truly sorry. If I hadn't done what I did, none of this would have happened, and you would probably be together now, married and—'

'Thanks, Michael, but that's not helping.' She rose, brushed imaginary crumbs from her skirt and kissed him on the cheek in farewell.

Shit, he'd forgotten how long that flight to Australia was. For James, though, it was luxury in his private plane chartered by another experienced pilot that allowed him to rest and sleep but mainly think. And there were many hours to think.

Turning into the main street of Canungra, it appeared to him like a pre-historic museum exhibit from the olden days. Passing The Outpost Café, he recalled the awesome strawberry milkshakes they used to make and of which he drank too many; the pub with its distinctive Tudor exterior that fed hundreds of tourists each Saturday lunch and the cute boutiques that lined the street, including the hairdresser and candy shop; the parks and green spaces. A sharp stab of something hit his chest, but he didn't know what it was. Nostalgia? Relief? Fond memories? Or perhaps a combination of all three.

He asked the cab to drop him at the factory. It was there he was called to first. Entering the shop at the front of the warehouse building on impulse, he purchased what used to be one of his favourites. A rough square-sized slab of peppermint dark chocolate. So simple, yet so delicious. The first bite and memories clawed at him, taking him back to being taught how to make the peppermint, mix it with the chocolate and allow it to set. He recalled every step. Then, practice to make the perfect batch, over and over. And teaching Sapphire when it was her turn. Taking another bite, the fresh mint flavour made his taste buds sing. At that moment, James believed wholeheartedly in the power of food transporting you.

In between mouthfuls, he ordered thousands of dollars worth of chocolate. The girl at the desk wasn't quite sure what was happening, and she had to source an especially large box for his goodies. It may well have been the biggest sale she'd ever made.

Letting the last remnants of chocolate melt on his tongue, he turned toward the back entry, where the offices used to be located, and the rear door to the factory. It was late, the world growing dim around him, and he hoped that Sapphire had left for the day. James would see her, but not yet. He needed to finish other business first.

The rear entry remained the same as in his memory. Simple milk crates overturned for seats, the concrete wall for support and an occasional table. If it was nostalgia, it was now hitting him square in the gut.

Pulling open the door, he entered the confined spaces. Seb was at his desk. Taking a deep breath, he went through and surprised the man.

'Jamie? Is that you?' Seb jumped out of his chair and moved around the desk to embrace him, old style, with a slap to the back before the proper hug began. Pulling apart, Seb held his shoulders, looked him up and down and said with a tear in his eye, 'It is so good to see you.'

'And you, too. I'm sorry it's been so long.'

Seb brushed aside his apologies. 'It's been tricky to follow your career but we understand you're a huge success and we could not be prouder.'

A knife stabbed James in the chest. This man would not be so welcoming when he knew the truth about the events all those years ago. During his time on the plane, James concluded that he didn't need to come clean only with Sapphie; on that list were also the factory and his former boss. He owed them.

'Let's celebrate,' Seb said. 'I'll get everyone together for dinner. Louisa will be delighted to see you.'

'No, not yet. I need to talk to you.' Jamie said, his voice devoid of humour and joviality.

'Okay.' Seb nodded but reached across his credenza to a tray of bottles and fine-cut crystal stout glasses. 'Yes, let's talk, but we will also drink.' And he poured generous nips of scotch. James gulped two down before he dared to proceed.

His old friend listened, nodded in the right places, and offered reassurance to continue. An hour later, they were well on their way to being drunk, but he'd done it, cleared the air and told the truth. The weight that had sat heavy on his chest, was lifted and he breathed easier.

'I always wondered,' Seb bowed his head. 'It didn't make sense. You were happy here; I knew you were. You were an integral part of our team. You loved and were loved. If you had said you wanted to go away and train and spread your wings, I would have understood. But it wasn't us, the factory; we could survive your departure; we had other staff, me,' he pointed to his chest, 'to keep the business going. It was Sapphire. You broke that poor girl's heart. She mourned you as though you had died. Her life stopped, and the joy sapped right out of her. That's why I sent her away to the mentorship, to rekindle the spark I knew grew inside of her. To reinvigorate some life in her. I wasn't aware I was sending her into your arms.'

'I am incredibly sorry for what happened. For what my father did. I was young and stupid and didn't know how to react or fix matters. I should have come to you, and we could have worked it out together; I realise that now. Instead, I fled from the scene of the crime. But now, I'm in a position to fix it. I can pay for any damages or hardship you suffered.'

Seb held up his palm. 'It was a long time ago, and we have moved on, prospered at times, and suffered at others. I do not want or need any compensation from you.'

They drank some more. 'For old times' sake, can you show me around? Tell me more about your ethical chocolate production and how it works?'

'Nothing would please me more.'

The windows on the second storey remained illuminated despite the late hour. Some small part of him hoped his father would be asleep, that he could put off this confrontation until another day.

Hopping into the ancient lift he was reminded of how stubborn his father was. After the accident, he'd tried to encourage him to relocate to a bottom-floor apartment, more manageable, with easy access for his chair. Flat refusal was the response, and ever since, they'd had to modify their living arrangements. Luckily, the building had a lift. In the early days, James wasn't able to sleep in fear of an emergency like a fire. How would he have gotten his one-hundred-kilogram father down the stairs? Sweat broke out on his brow at old memories and forgotten fears. He hadn't thought about that issue for a long time. Out of sight, out of mind?

At the front door, he searched under the pot plant for the spare key. Would it still be there? But his fingers found the cool metallic surface with its grooves, and he let himself into the unit.

Upon entry, he heard the buzz of the television and the dull glow emanating from his father's bedroom. The carer would have arrived hours earlier and helped him to bed, and there he would stay until assisted again in the morning. Those old feelings of despondency returned. What sort of life did his father lead with his severe restrictions? It had been a burden he'd carried after the accident, but upon his father's betrayal, it'd been easy to forget. Now, it was impossible not to worry when confronted with the reality of his father's situation once more.

'Dad?' he called out tentatively, his hand still holding the door open, not wanting to frighten his father with its resounding bang as it shut. A pause, the TV muted.

'Son? Jamie?'

Entering the bedroom, he saw a diminutive man, shrunken

with age, hair greying at the temples, wearing a white Bonds singlet, and lounging upon the pillows. Despite everything, his father had retained his dazzling good looks and James couldn't help but smile.

'Son,' his father repeated. James approached the bed and as if acting on rote, as if his father's action hadn't torn their relationship apart five years ago, as if they'd seen each other yesterday, he hugged the bulky man and clutched him tight. At the sensation of his father's chest heaving, James fought back his own tears until they fell silently onto the man and dampened the white sheets; he let them fall.

James and Michael didn't sleep much. They talked through the evening until the sun commenced its ascent and the day began to dawn. James woke now next to his father in the double bed, the sun creeping through the open curtains. His father snored softly, covered by the bed sheets, and tucked in; James was on top of the blanket, fully dressed, lying where he'd landed, and he even still wore his shoes.

Rising as quietly as possible, he tugged the curtains closed and the room was once again swallowed by darkness. 'Dad, Dad,' he said, gently shaking his father's shoulders. 'I'm heading out for a while. Do you need anything before I go? Bathroom?'

His father shook his head and told him to go, and James tucked the covers tightly around him. Exiting the bedroom, he made a decision. It had been so easy to ignore his father after what he'd done, but looking around his apartment, whilst clean and neat and providing for everything he needed, it wasn't good enough. He'd purchase a new home for him. Canungra was one of the most beautiful parts of Queensland and his father had no view of the rolling, verdant hills outside, or any view at all.

James was planning to do a lot of things, but first, he needed to see Sapphie.

Chapter Twenty-Three

It was Saturday. Sapphire had been home a week and her family kept acting on tenterhooks around her, as if at any moment she might snap in half. Hadn't her foray across the world proven to everyone that she was stronger than she'd thought? That she could tough things out and survive? Manage. It was Jamie, she knew, his sudden and unexpected return to her life that had them worried. And then, of course, the bombshell of what his father had told her.

Okay, she'd admit she went into a slump immediately after. What girl wouldn't? It was a lot to take in, and she didn't, couldn't know what it meant other than providing an explanation of what had occurred all those years ago and providing a reason Jamie had left. But she maintained that if he'd really loved her, he wouldn't have left or at the very least, he would have been honest and confided in her. So, in fact, nothing had changed, had it?

Her decision on that long, lonely flight home, cramped into

economy next to a large man who took up half of her seat space, had been to get on with things. Such an easy catch cry! Sapphire Banks would live up to her bold name, finally and get on with her life. It wasn't as if she had a choice, was it? Give up or keep going. She'd acted tough in Hallstatt, had to protect herself in front of Jamie, and she'd been proud of herself too, but the fact was she'd never stop loving that infuriating man. But what she had to learn was to get over him. Love him and acknowledge same—to herself anyway—and simply get on with things. Make the most of the opportunities and try to let down some barriers. So not only did she have to prove it to herself, but she also had to reassure her family that she wasn't the fragile, dispirited *nothing* she'd been upon departure. And she'd start today.

'Mum, I'll set up cabin five. You have the newlyweds arriving tonight, right?' she addressed her mother.

'Oh, darling, you don't have to do that one. Cabin three is checking out after the week, you can clean that one?' her mother volunteered with a crooked smile, trying to conceal her concern.

'No, I'd much rather set up than clean up. It'll be fun.'

'Okay, if you're sure.' Yeah, she was getting tired of the wrap-me-in-cottonwool scenario currently playing out at home.

She kissed her Gran on the forehead, called for Winston and headed off.

The six cabins were within short walking distance from the main house. Enjoying the crisp morning air and the dappled sun, she ambled, pulling along a trolley of items she needed and letting Winston sniff at things of interest along the way.

At the cabin, she unfastened the windows to let the fresh air flow, played some soft music in the background and let Winston curl up on an old blanket in the corner while she got to work.

What did romantic couples deeply in love want? The chilling champagne was easy; two bottles were on ice in the bar fridge. She laid out fresh towels, soaps, and luxury items in the bathroom and placed hand-picked fresh flowers in the main room and a vase next to the basin in the bathroom. Now for the fun part: the rose petals. The four-poster bed had crisp white linen and bedspread and hospital corners. On the white back-drop, she created a love heart of red, pink and purple petals. It looked magnificent, and a pain shot across her chest. But hey, that was normal, right? Any single girl setting up love hearts made of flowers was bound to shed a tear. Who didn't want to arrive to this after having declared your true love to your betrothed?

Then she scattered petals into the bath and around the floor. If nothing else, the smell was divine. Sapphire quickly shut the windows to prevent petals from skittering out of place. And the pièce de résistance, a wicker basket of goodies – fresh baguette stick, water crackers, fruit and of course, Hinterland Chocolate. Placing them into the perfect arrangement, she fondled the chocolate wrapper. Maybe Hinterland packaging was sort of old-fashioned and outdated. It was quaint in its clear plastic wrap and gingham-style check sticker advertising the flavour. The newest addition: the sticker advertising their ethical sourcing and production of chocolate.

Winston, who'd been sound asleep, suddenly leapt up and raced out of the room before plodding down the front stairs. He'd be okay; he knew these fields as well as she and would wander back after a play.

Instead, a heavier tread bounded up the stairs, nothing like the scuttle of Winston's little paws across the front decking and timber flooring. Perhaps her mother had come to check on her? Sapphire controlled her sigh.

She turned, plastering a smile on her face, expecting her mother, but there stood Jamie. Her mouth hung open, and for a moment, she forgot where she was. She couldn't be in Canungra because Jamie would not be in their hick hometown. He lived in continental Europe in one of the prettiest places on Earth, miles from here, miles from her.

But he spoke, and it was him.

'You've been expecting me then?' he smiled and gestured to the room, which Sapphire had to admit looked incredibly welcoming and warm and, yes, romantic.

'What? No,' she stammered, not quite getting the joke in the shock of standing here with Jamie.

'What, what are you doing here?'

Winston demanded attention and jumped up and down up on Jamie's legs. He crouched down to him and rubbed his tummy when he lay on his back, fondled his ears, scratched where he loved being tickled. Eventually, he rose and brought the dog with him, holding him close.

'I've missed you, Winston,' he murmured to the dog.

'Oh, how is Winnie?' she jumped in, remembering the gorgeous puppy.

'She's great. Missing you, of course. But you'll be pleased to know that she is wandering the factory shamelessly as if she owns it and going home each night with someone different.'

'Oh,' Sapphire uttered. That wasn't what she wanted at all.

'Upon my return, she'll live with me and I'll take her into the office each day.'

Oh, yes, she wanted that, but he'd only just arrived and to talk of home, his home, already. Well...

'Your dad told me...' she started.

'I'm so sorry...'

They both spoke simultaneously and then clammed up, suddenly aware they were alone, together, and so much had happened, and where did you start?

'Can we sit and talk?' She nodded, and they headed outside and sat on the bottom step and threw sticks to Winston, who provided a vital distraction from the words.

'I owe you an explanation.'

'Your dad told me when I got back.'

'He did?'

'Yes, I'm so sorry that happened; it was a shitty thing to do.'

'Please don't apologise to me. You have nothing to be sorry for. I ran away. I was frightened, afraid, embarrassed and full of shame at what he did. Shocked he would behave like that after everything I'd done for him when he knew how important Hinterland was to me.' Jamie paused and shook his head. 'But we don't need to rehash that. I've seen my dad, and we've talked it through. He was experiencing a tough time and acted out of character. He's desperately sorry and has cleaned up his act, so I'm proud of him and very sorry for how I've treated him.'

'That's good; I'm happy you've cleared the air. I won't excuse his behaviour, but he loves you.'

Jamie nodded. "But Sapphie, what I did to you.' He looked away across the field and threw Winston another stick. 'I was such a child, running away like that, avoiding facing those around me, facing the consequences. I sincerely thought I could run away and the whole sorry mess would be forgotten, I'd be forgotten, and more importantly, I thought I was protecting all of you from my dad because if I left, he'd have no more information to sell because I wouldn't be feeding him anything. And how could I confess that my own father had stolen the information I'd given him and profited? I was so embarrassed. So, at the time, as stupid as it sounds, I thought I was doing the right thing. I needed desperately to fix it and thought I had the perfect plan.'

'I loved you. We had a future. You very quickly threw that away.' Sapphire couldn't look at him either and it was her turn to carefully consider the fields surrounding them. All that hurt couldn't be expressed in one sentence.

'I'm so sorry. I never stopped loving you,' he snuck a quick glance at her. 'I know I left in terrible circumstances, but I truly never stopped loving you. I didn't leave because of you; I left to help you. I haven't loved anyone since.' She arched a brow at this. Perhaps he hadn't loved, but he'd had fun or at least perhaps tried to love someone else, which was more than she had.

He turned to face her now, reached for her hands and clasped them. 'Can you forgive me? I would completely understand if you said no and pushed me away; that the hurt cuts too deep, that you hate me.'

'That's the problem, I guess, I do forgive you, have forgiven you. And that makes me mad at myself. Makes me weak. I want to hate you,' her voice cracked. 'I really do. What you did was rotten. You destroyed our future together, the lives we'd planned and up and left. I do forgive you and I still love you, but I wish I didn't. I wish I'd found someone else who adored me, cared for me, cherished me, and lived happily ever after in their arms, and you were a distant memory.' Tears slowly found their way down her cheeks.

Jamie inched closer. 'I will adore you, cherish you, live with you and love you every day. I want us to live out our future together, making the chocolate we'd always dreamed of.'

'We never imagined living in Hallstatt, making foreign chocolate. We were living here in simple Canungra making Hinterland chocolate.'

'Dreams and plans can change, can't they? If you are prepared to give me a second chance, I'd make sacrifices for you. I'll live here and work back at Hinterland if you say that's the deal, I would!' he declared at the first hint of a smile on the corner of her lips.

'James White, are you saying you will do anything I say?' The use of his full name was not lost on either of them.

'Let's not get carried away,' he said but matched her grin. 'What I'm saying, is that together we plan the next steps.'

Sapphire watched Winston bounding like a rabbit through the long grass, at the rising hills surrounding them. 'But what happens when things get tough again? Will you flee each time it gets too hard?'

'No, of course not! I won't ever do that again.'

'Jamie, it's been over five years. You haven't come to these realisations before now?'

'Honestly, I put home and Australia and my past out of my mind. I never thought about it because it was too painful. But when you arrived, you brought each agonising memory back. And when I saw you, it hurt how much I'd missed you. The first time you turned up in my kitchen, I wanted to reach across and hold you, caress you, feel and smell your skin. I almost couldn't control myself. And then, that night in Zermatt, oh my God, that was torture!'

'But why didn't you?'

'It was two things. It was sort of like admitting defeat that I hadn't forged this incredible new life that I had worked so hard at establishing when I was suddenly longing for the past. A past I ran from. And then, of course, the way I left. How do you make amends after that? But it was when you left, I knew then when you weren't there, near me, how much you meant to me, and I could no longer deny it, and I realised I couldn't live without you anymore. And no matter what it took, I had to make things right.'

Sapphire didn't bother to wipe away the tears rolling down her cheeks or stop the sniffle because her nose was running. Jamie reached into a bag and extracted her bangle and she cried harder. He reached for her arm and gently placed it back in its rightful spot. 'Please don't ever take it off again.'

Her fingers immediately went to the smooth surface of gold and caressed it like an old friend. The world tilted slightly back to rights.

He pulled something else out of a bag. 'I have gifts for you.' Sapphire held up her hands in protest.

'No, don't, let me be kind to you. I want to spoil you and give you presents every day. Please let me love you.'

She covered his mouth with her hand. 'The only present I want is you by my side, committed, with me.'

He leaned forward then, their eyes linked, and she met him, their lips a breath away from each other. Sapphire felt the heat of his mouth, the intensity of his eyes that explored hers, seeking, questioning until she shut hers and their mouths connected.

Her stomach swooped with joy as she tasted him once more. It was different, time had etched itself upon both of them, and whilst their mouths were demanding with heat and need and desire, there was a restraint, a newness, a recognition that things were different.

Winston licked their feet and drew them apart. They laughed. Jamie placed the carefully wrapped, beautiful, hard box with a white label in cursive writing in her hand. The label read *House of Joubert*. She inhaled the scent of lavender, mixed with deeper traces of spice and a hint of floral. Extracting the exquisite pink glass bottle, she hugged him and thanked him.

'This is a bottle of perfume from the best perfumer in France. Do you like it?'

Holding the Eau de Parfum to her nose, she inhaled. 'It's divine.'

Now, he gave her a purple drawstring bag. 'This is a declaration of my love for you. Of my commitment to you and me. I love you Sapphie, and by forgiving me, I vow to do better, to love you with everything I've got, never to run away and always be honest. Thank you for giving me another chance. I will not let you down.' He left it for her to untie and extract a velvet-covered box matching the shade of the bag. Her heart started beating too fast in her chest as she opened it. 'Oh my, Jamie, it's too much, I can't. It's . . . it's—'

'Beautiful, right? Like you. May I?' and he indicated placing the ring on her finger.

She paused him again. 'It's too much, too soon, I can't, we can't.'

'Sapphie.' He covered her hands with his. 'It's okay, I agree. We must get to know each other again. We will get married one day, but we don't have to do it yet, straight away. We will take our time; I will wait until you trust me again and when you are ready. Until then, you can wear this ring. It is from the best jeweller in Spain, *Blanco Fine Jewels*.'

Jamie placed it onto her right-hand ring finger. It was a large square-set pink diamond on a thick gold band covered with hundreds of tiny clear diamonds. It glistened, and it sparkled. It was big, it was bold, and it was beautiful, and she might never take it off.

'Thank you. I love you too.' Holding Winston up between them, he licked their faces as they kissed again.

Epilogue

Twelve months later

'Smile, sweetie,' Sapphire said to James as she held up her phone between them to take a selfie. They sat in luxury seats on their private jet plane about to head to their coffee farms in East Africa. James relaxed as someone else charted the flight. Sapphire snapped the image and said, 'I'll send this to Marcus to load on the page.'

James agreed.

Marcus had hung around—in his own words, where else would he go—and was now the head of their PR and marketing division. He was loyal, committed and doing a fabulous job. As an added bonus, he'd met and fallen in love with a local tourist operator, Josef, and was happier than ever. About six months ago, Lina had resurfaced, asking for her old job back, apologising, saying what a huge mistake she'd made. Sapphire would have given her another chance; she was like that, but James was adamant. In the interim, Marcus took on the role with relish.

Now, Lina had only been spotted on the Instagram pages of a small, unknown chocolate shop, but they wished her well.

Winnie jumped from Sapphire's lap and into her own custom-made seat for the flight. Right next to Winston's bed. Upon their return from Australia, it was never an option to leave behind Winston, and he'd adjusted to life in Hallstatt with the help of his best friend, Winnie. James and Sapphire, along with the rest of the Grindelwald team doted on those dogs. There was a new range of ideas floating around based on the shape of the dogs and their gorgeous furry faces on the label. They were sure it was going to be an instant best seller.

'Hey, have you checked the latest sales figures?' Sapphire asked James as he read the daily paper spread out in his lap.

'No, not yet. How do they look?'

'It's the best since the transition. We might have got through the worst of it. Sales are definitely up.'

His whole face spread into a smile, his eyes lighting up. Even now, after all this time, Sapphire still found his grin irresistible, and she reached for his hand. 'I'm so pleased. It was a risk, but it paid off in the longer term. And it's worth it, right?'

James kissed her hand. 'Absolutely, once I became aware of the true plight of the situation, there was no option. But we must keep things on course at the farms, too.' In the last twelve months, James had purchased large tracks of land suitable for cacao bean farming on the Ivory Coast. Purchasing and transforming the land had been the easy part. Keeping the locals honest and the children away from harvesting had been harder. They wanted to hire and employ local workers. Still, they'd had to pay both Australian and European workers well to oversee the ventures and ensure they stuck to their ethical sourcing brand

and absolute abhorrence of child slave labour. Frequently, they visited the farms to make their presence known, and to check on their fabulous produce and to ensure it was maintained to their usual high quality. James also met with the local government representatives to ensure that everyone on the ground was happy.

'I cannot wait to get home.' After Africa, they were heading to Australia.

'Me, too. I'm looking forward to seeing Dad settled in his new place. The photos look amazing.'

'I also can't wait to talk to the architect and check out the designs for our house.' Childhood excitement bubbled over. Her parents had gifted them a parcel of land on their property for them to build their dream home. During this stay, they'd hole up in one of the cabins near where they'd build and dream of what might be.

'We've got so much to do on this trip,' she murmured.

'Yeah, we do, but Hinterland has been in great hands. You'll probably find there's very little work there. We're just the big hobnobs coming into land and getting in their way.'

'Seb won't agree, and the local girls will go all gooey-eyed at the rich and famous boss arriving.' She giggled.

For Sapphie, and to save Hinterland and ensure its long-term survival, James had made Seb an offer he couldn't refuse, along with his entire team, on the condition Seb stayed in charge of day-to-day operations.

'Will they be okay with what we have planned?'

'Change is always hard,' he acknowledged, 'but this is only planning for a bigger and better factory with modern machines and appliances and a proper space for staff to enjoy their break and some luxury. Everyone at Hinterland has worked hard for so long and in mediocre conditions. This will provide them with the treatment they deserve.'

Sapphire agreed and she thought, after they realised the potential and the benefits, the team at Hinterland, Seb mainly, would also agree. And given that their sales had been exponential in the last twelve months, the mood would be jovial. They were an example of a company doing the right thing, weathering the storm of the pandemic and price hikes but maintaining their high ethical and moral ground and producing only the very best chocolate made from beans sourced from farms that paid their staff well and did not take advantage of the local community. It was possible.

'I also can't wait to get back on the line. Make some chocolate!' she exclaimed. 'These next six months are going to fly. I'm not going to miss the vicious European winter in Hallstatt this year!'

As a pledge to each other and to maintain their connection to Australia, Sapphire and James had committed to six months each year in both Hallstatt and Australia. They stayed in Europe for their magnificent summer season and returned to Australia when the days shortened and the temperature dipped, thereby achieving the best of both worlds. They would never tire of the heat of the Australian summer.

'And I cannot wait to tell them our exciting news.' Sapphire gently nursed her tummy where a little life was growing. James beamed back at her; their love, achievements, teamwork, and hard work had come to fruition.

Sapphire Banks was finally living up to her bold name.

Acknowledgments

Thank you so much for diving back into the world of these exotic millionaires and travelling to Austria and Switzerland this time. My family enjoyed a long European trip years ago and one of our favourite places was Hallstatt. You never know when these towns might pop up in your writing and here it is. It is just as idyllic as it sounds and one of the most beautiful European destinations to visit.

Thank you to early reader, Leigh, to Annie Seaton for her amazing editorial skills, Emma Powell of EJP Covers for the fantastic cover (I can't wait until you see the four books together!) and to Blurbs by Bel, AKA Belinda Williams for her invaluable help with the back cover blurb.

Can't wait to see you in Tuscany! Thanks once again for reading.

About the Author

Leanne Lovegrove is a lawyer, wife and mother and a lover of romance and reading. Her law career created an addiction to coffee but provides countless story ideas. She is the author of romantic fiction novels. Leanne writes sweeping love stories with happily-ever-afters with strong female heroines and often set in the beautiful landscape of Australia. This is the third in her European Tycoon series. This time she has left the shores of Australia behind for the exotic climes of various European cities for romances with dashing Tycoons. She lives in Brisbane, Australia with her husband and three children.

Other books in the European Tycoon series

The Spanish Jeweller (European Tycoons #1)

REVIEWS FOR THE FRENCH PERFUMER

WOW! I loved this book so much I couldn't put it down, dinner and drinks were done one handed all night! The setting and characters o this book were divine, I felt like I was there and could really smell the roses so to speak! Full of love, loss and overcoming trauma were all done so delicately, really pulled at the heartstrings. Loved everything about it and cannot wait for the next book in this scrumptious series - Karina, Goodreads

I loved this one so much and my trip to France, another fabulously written story…fabulous characters, emotionally filled story and one that I would highly recommend. I am already looking forward to the next book in the series – Helen Sibbrit, reviewer

The delightful setting and beautiful descriptions of floral fields and dazzling locations offer lawyers of extra sensory stimulation. For me, the icing on the cake was the delicious pink-tinged descriptions and references to the colour of love…a very inviting and vicariously sensory read – Chrissie Belbrae

I loved this fairy-tale like story that flowed along like a dream…it ends on a high note of sweetly scented, passion and promise. Hats off to Leanne for another delightful journey to the world of the rich and famous. The character development is perfect, the story length just right and the plot has enough turns and surprises. This story will make your skin tingle, your nose awaken to delightful scents and your heart bursting with love and joy – Cindy L Spear, reviewer and blogger

The Italian Winemaker (European Tycoons #4)
Coming soon!

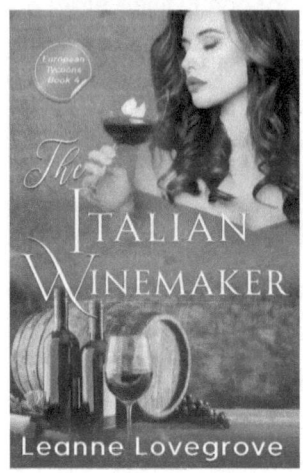

To find out more about Leanne's books, you can find her here:

Leanne's website: www.leannelovegroveauthor.com

OR

facebook.com/leanne.lovegrove.545

instagram.com/leannelovegroveauthor

bookbub.com/profile/leanne-lovegrove

Also by Leanne Lovegrove

Leanne's other novels:

Unexpected Delivery

Illegal Love

Keeper of the Light

A Good Life

Her Outback Home

Bellethorpe Series:

Love In Between (novella #1)

Caught In Between (novella #2)

Bellethorpe In Between Boxset (novellas #1 and #2)

Buried In Between novel #4

Novellas

Escapades of a Personal Stylist

Love on the Sweeping Plains

Anthologies

Love in a Sunburnt Land Vol 1

Love in a Sunburnt Land Vol 2